# DECEPTIVE TRUTHS

DeAnna Julie Dodson

*Annie's*®
AnniesFiction.com

## Books in the Sweet Intrigue series

*Betrayal of Trust*
*Burning Danger*
*Christmas Peril*
*Dangerous at Heart*
*Web of Lies*
*Deceptive Truths*
*Fatal Waters*
*Gathering Storms*
*Under Suspicion*

*. . . and more to come!*

Library of Congress-in-Publication Data
*Deceptive Truths* / by DeAnna Julie Dodson
p. cm.
I. Title
2021931469

AnniesFiction.com
(800) 282-6643
Annie's Sweet Intrigue™
Series Creator: Shari Lohner
Editor: Lorie Jones

10 11 12 13 14 | Printed in China | 9 8 7 6 5 4 3 2 1

Cooper Cole huffed in frustration as traffic ground to a stop. Again. Even at ten o'clock on a Thursday night, it wasn't usually this slow. He assumed there was an accident somewhere ahead of him on the expressway. Things always got weird when there was a full moon.

He sighed, nudged his car forward a few inches, and turned up his police scanner. He had left the force nearly a year ago, and listening to the calls—with the familiar code numbers, addresses, and voices—sometimes gave him a twinge of regret. He still felt a bond with the guys he'd worked with, the brass, and the neighborhood he'd protected and served.

Deep Ellum, an arts and entertainment district in East Dallas, shouted its quirky presence to the world with bright graffiti-style murals. The area contained art galleries, clubs, restaurants, shops, theaters, and old warehouses converted into pricey apartments. Cooper enjoyed the colorful mixture of people from all walks of life who thrived here, but even though he still lived nearby, he didn't always seem to be a part of it anymore. He often felt like a visitor, but he came out this way when he could. Usually for the music.

Tonight Cooper was heading to a club to hear his friend Brandon Marley perform with his band. Cooper and Brandon had been friends since sixth grade, almost twenty years ago, and anytime Brandon was playing in Deep Ellum, Cooper tried to make it to his show.

Cooper was about to switch off the scanner and put on one of Brandon's CDs when he heard the dispatcher's voice.

"Charlie 599, report of random gunfire," Jayla Randall said.

Cooper winced when he heard her voice. Of course he'd heard Jayla on the scanner off and on over the past few months, but knowing that she was working dispatch tonight of all nights made him feel uneasy. It was May 7, exactly one year since everything had changed.

Cooper didn't have to close his eyes to see Jayla clearly—long, light-brown hair, wide green eyes surrounded by thick lashes, rosy cheeks that dimpled when she smiled. He remembered how she came up exactly to his chin and how she fit so perfectly in his arms as if she had been made to be there. He still didn't know if his decisions following what had happened a year ago had been the correct ones. Was she really better off without him? He knew he wasn't better off without her.

He returned his attention to the scanner.

Charlie 599 gave his location through a burst of static.

"10-4," Jayla said. "Charlie 502, can I get a case number?"

"That would be 1-1-9-1-8-6."

"1-1-9-1-8-6," Jayla repeated. "10-4."

The police station wasn't far from Cooper's current location. Traffic was picking up speed a little, and he toyed with the idea of dropping by for a minute. While Jayla was working, she wouldn't be able to do more than give him a smile, if she was willing to do even that. But maybe some of the guys he knew would be there too. Seeing a few familiar faces might help him shake the uneasy feeling that had come over him when he'd first heard her voice.

Cooper didn't know what was bothering him. It wasn't as if he hadn't thought of that particular night every day since then. And he had certainly thought of Jayla.

He hadn't actually considered until then the kind of stress 911 operators had to deal with. It was always urgent, and often it was a life-and-death situation. He knew now that it could also be terrifying. He didn't blame Jayla for transferring from 911 operator to police dispatch.

Cooper knew that tonight Jayla would be thinking of what had happened a year ago. But did that mean she'd want to see him? If she did, would his presence make those memories better or worse?

When he thought about it, it would probably be a shock for her. He would go and listen to Brandon play. That was what he had come here for, and that was what he was going to do. Jayla didn't need him turning up like the proverbial bad penny. Not tonight. He reached to switch off the scanner.

"Charlie 587," Jayla said. She paused, then relayed an address.

Cooper froze, his hand in midair. He recognized that address. Was he hearing things? And had he imagined the tremor in her voice?

"10-4," Charlie 587 said.

"587, the victim is in apartment four," Jayla added.

"No," Cooper said, gripping the steering wheel. He suddenly noticed that the car in front of him had stopped. He had to slam on his brakes to keep from hitting it.

It couldn't be. Not that particular apartment on that street. Not tonight. What was happening there? Why hadn't Jayla said what the call was about?

The car behind him tapped its horn, and he realized there was a two-car gap between himself and the car ahead. He closed it quickly, waiting for something more from the scanner.

There was a burst of static, and he was sure he could hear Jayla's voice in it, but he couldn't make out the words.

"Come on," he muttered, cranking up the volume. "What's the call?"

"Say again, dispatch," Charlie 587 said. "You're breaking up."

"10-4, 587," Jayla said, and this time her voice was crystal clear. "The call is a suspected homicide."

Cooper couldn't believe his ears. It had to be a mistake. How could there be a second murder in the same apartment where there had been one exactly a year ago today?

Jayla Randall sat at her computer, still staring at the 911 call she had just dispatched. It was another murder.

It was her worst nightmare all over again.

Jayla had been working as a 911 operator exactly one year ago. She had answered a call, only to hear a woman's terrified whisper that chilled her to her bones.

"A man is coming for me right now. He's going to kill me. He wants to make me sorry for what I did to him."

When the woman had given her address, Jayla had requested immediate assistance.

A moment later, Jayla had heard the door burst open and the rattle of the phone as the woman dropped it. To her horror, Jayla had been forced to listen to every moment of terror and pain until the woman's eventual death.

Then Jayla had heard pounding on the door, muffled shouts of the police trying to get in, and gunshots. At the time, Jayla hadn't known that the man she loved had been shot in the head. She hadn't known that one second would take Cooper Cole from her as effectively as if he had been killed.

Earlier today, before this call had come in, she had thought about Cooper as well as the murder of Jill Kinner. Did this day mean anything to him? For her, it meant the beginning of the end. She had forced herself not to get in touch with him because she knew it was too late.

Jayla shook her head. She needed to pull herself together. She had an important job to do.

"Charlie 587 calling dispatch. 587 to dispatch. Come in."

"Go ahead, 587," Jayla said. Somehow her voice didn't shake, but her hands did.

"Dispatch, we're going to need Officer Stanley out here on the case and a forensics team."

"Roger, 587," Jayla answered. "Will dispatch."

"Thanks. 587 out."

It was the same as last year, except that this time she didn't have to hear the murder firsthand. But she couldn't help wondering if last year's killer had struck again.

Cooper had to go to the apartment and see what was going on. He was almost at the exit.

A few minutes later, traffic began moving again. He noticed the red glow of flares up ahead and the lights of emergency vehicles that indicated an accident, but it seemed to be in the last stages of cleanup.

He managed to get to the exit with reasonable ease, and it wasn't long before he reached the two-story clapboard apartment house. It was painted robin's-egg blue with cream-colored trim, and it featured redbrick columns and a wide front porch. The house had been built in the thirties. Then in the nineties, it had been renovated and divided into four apartments, each one offering elegant amenities, a small amount of space, and high rent.

Two police cars were already parked in front, their lights flashing red and blue. Cooper recognized Officer David Stanley walking away from one of the cars. He pulled up to the curb, rolled down his window, and called out to the officer.

Stanley squinted, then strode over to him and raised his eyebrows. "What are you doing here? I thought you were done with the force and had become a private investigator."

Cooper shut off the engine and got out of the car. "I heard about the suspected homicide on my scanner, and I had to check it out. You know how it is."

Stanley shook his hand. "I haven't been inside yet, but it's quite a coincidence, isn't it?"

"Copycat?" Cooper asked, appraising the illuminated house. There was light in every window, and it was streaming out the open front door.

"Maybe."

"It can't be Dane Wolff again," Cooper said. "He's been locked up for nearly a year."

Last year, Mrs. Eleanor Calvin, the landlady, had told the police that Dane Wolff rented apartment four, and his name was on the lease. But Jill Kinner, the victim, lived in the apartment. Wolff paid the rent and was a frequent visitor. He was the one who had murdered Jill.

"That's true," Stanley said. He motioned to the front door. "I'm going inside. Do you want to come?"

Cooper nodded, glad for the invitation. Texas was hot in May, even at night.

"Daniels and Kent are in there already," Stanley said.

Cooper had worked with Brad Daniels on the force, but he didn't know the other officer. "Who's Kent? A rookie?"

Stanley nodded. "He's turning into a good officer. Daniels has been showing him the ropes."

Cooper was glad to hear it. He respected Daniels.

"It might help if you take a look around and see if there's anything you remember from last time."

Cooper flashed back to last year. He had been on patrol when he'd received a call that there was a domestic violence incident in progress at this address in apartment four. He'd been too late to save Jill Kinner. Guilt and regret crashed down on him, and he almost stumbled under the oppressive weight.

"Are you okay?" Stanley asked as he placed a hand on Cooper's shoulder.

Cooper flinched, then blinked into the quiet, dark night. He reminded himself that it was today, not a year ago. "Yeah, I'm okay."

Stanley studied Cooper for a moment before leading the way to the house.

Cooper followed him up the porch steps and into the foyer. Mindful of the air-conditioning, he shut the door behind them, then glanced around. He remembered there had been pictures on the walls, a ficus tree in one corner, and a long, narrow bench under the stairway landing. All of that was gone now, and the foyer was bare. It appeared that the place was being stripped down for remodeling.

Mrs. Eleanor Calvin, a wizened toffee-skinned woman in her late seventies, stood in her doorway of apartment one, arms crossed. The landlady wore a powder-blue robe and a gray scarf wound around her hair. The woman hadn't changed a bit. She was as slight and peppery as before, barely coming up to Cooper's shoulder.

"They told me you weren't with the police anymore," Mrs. Calvin said, eyeing Cooper. "After what happened last year."

"I'm not," he said, "but they thought I might be able to help in this case since I was here before."

Mrs. Calvin pursed her lips. "Katie's dead, isn't she." It wasn't a question.

"I haven't been up there yet, ma'am," Cooper responded.

The wail of a siren announced the arrival of the paramedics.

"We'll talk to you again soon," Stanley said to Mrs. Calvin.

Cooper and Stanley followed the paramedics up the stairs and into apartment four.

The paramedics rushed over to the victim and got to work, but Cooper was afraid it was too late to do anything for the young woman sprawled on the floor.

Daniels and another man met Cooper and Stanley at the door.

"This is a surprise," Daniels said to Cooper. "Why are you here?"

Cooper explained that he'd heard the call on the scanner.

"He came here out of concern," Stanley added, "and I invited him to check out the scene since he was here last time."

Daniels introduced Cooper to Troy Kent. With his wide blue eyes and mop of dark hair, Kent appeared every inch the eager young rookie.

The forensics team arrived, and they began taking photos and examining the scene. Stanley and the other two officers joined the team and started investigating.

Cooper stayed off to the side, lost in thought. On the night of the first murder last year, he hadn't had a chance to go inside the apartment. As he'd braced himself in preparation for breaking the door down, it had flown open, and he'd been flung against the wall with an explosion of sound and pain. The killer had burst out of the door, shot Cooper, then charged past him down the stairs and into the night.

Cooper had been able to hold on to consciousness for only a few minutes after that. He remembered Mrs. Calvin holding his hand, tears sliding down her lined cheeks as she asked the Lord to help him. That was all he could recall until he woke up in the hospital.

Weeks later, after Cooper had gotten out of the hospital, he had returned to the scene of the crime and had finally entered apartment four. Scanning the place this time, he realized that it had been remodeled. He wondered if it was slated to be remodeled yet again, like the rest of the house.

Stanley returned to Cooper. "From what I can see, it's the same MO as last time. This victim was shot exactly like the other one was."

Cooper felt his stomach clench. He didn't want to know the details. Not yet anyway. He'd had enough the first time.

"Are you okay?" Stanley asked.

"Sure," Cooper said, trying to pull himself together.

"Did you notice anything from last time?"

"No, the apartment has been remodeled since I was here last."

"Let's go talk to Mrs. Calvin," Stanley said.

They went downstairs to the landlady's apartment, and Stanley knocked.

Mrs. Calvin opened the door immediately.

"I'm sorry, but she's dead," Stanley said.

"I'll tell you what," Mrs. Calvin said, her mouth tightening. "I never had trouble before what happened last year, and then everything was fine again until tonight. It's not right."

"May we come in, ma'am?" Stanley asked, pushing the door open a little wider. "We need to ask you a few questions."

The woman nodded and stepped back, a glimmer of tears in her dark eyes. "Would you like some coffee?"

Cooper and Stanley thanked her.

Mrs. Calvin ushered them inside. "Please excuse the mess. I've sold this place, and I'm moving as fast as I can. The buyer had a scheduling problem with the contractors, so they gave me a nice bonus to let them start immediately."

Cooper glanced around her apartment. It wasn't as empty as the foyer was. The furniture was still in place, but the shelves and tabletops were bare. There was a stack of boxes along the front wall that almost obscured the wide window.

"That's great," Stanley said. "Did you have any problems getting the tenants to vacate?"

"I already had apartment two vacant, and the young man in number three moved out when he heard I'd sold the place," Mrs. Calvin answered. "Poor Katie didn't want to leave, but she was packing up already too. Her movers were supposed to come on Saturday, same as mine. Now I suppose it'll all have to go into storage."

"Once we've finished with the scene," Stanley told her.

The two men followed her to the kitchen table and sat down. Mrs. Calvin rummaged in a box and got out three china cups with an old-fashioned rose pattern and filled them from the pot still in the coffee maker. Then she set a sugar bowl and a cream pitcher, both in the same pattern, in the middle of the table. "Help yourselves," she said as she joined them at the table.

"Sorry to put you to so much trouble," Cooper said.

Mrs. Calvin snorted. "I'm not packing up all my coffee things till I'm ready to walk out that door for the last time."

Cooper waited until she had added cream and sugar to her coffee before he fixed his own with lots of cream, no sugar.

"What can you tell us about tonight?" Stanley asked. He took a sip of his black coffee.

Mrs. Calvin drew a shuddering breath. She suddenly appeared as delicate as the china cup in her hands. "I don't know. It's too horrible to have this happen here again."

Cooper put his hand over hers. "I realize it's a terrible situation, but we need your help to find out who did this."

"Can you tell us anything about the victim?" Stanley asked.

Mrs. Calvin took a handkerchief from her pocket and dabbed at her eyes. "Her name was Katie Myers. Katherine was how she signed the lease, but she went by Katie."

"Did she live alone?" Cooper asked.

"Yes, and she lived quietly," she said. "She didn't have people in and out at all hours. Went to church most Sundays."

Stanley took out a tablet and started making notes. "Was she a loner?"

"I'd say she was more of a worker than a loner," Mrs. Calvin replied. "She had her friends over sometimes, but mostly she didn't have time for partying. She worked as a cashier while she went to school. She was getting her nursing degree. She told me she was almost done."

"Was she seeing anybody?" Stanley asked, pausing over his tablet. "Anybody regular?"

"No one she told me about. She went out some, sometimes out to one of the clubs to hear the music. She liked jazz. It was one of the things we talked about when she'd stop in. She went on dates, but I think she was too busy to focus on any one man."

"How often did you talk to her?" Stanley asked.

"She'd have coffee or tea with me every so often," she said. "It was usually when she came to pay her rent."

"When she went out, did she ever mention a particular name?" Cooper asked, but he wasn't sure it mattered. This was already too much like what had happened the year before. He didn't even know many of the facts yet, but there was something in the whole atmosphere of the case that turned him inside out. And then there was the date—May 7.

"What?" he asked when he realized Stanley and Mrs. Calvin were both staring at him expectantly. "I'm sorry. I guess I got distracted."

She pursed her lips. "I said there wasn't any name I can remember. If Katie mentioned any, it was only in passing, and I can't recall there was ever the same one twice. I think if she had been seeing anybody she genuinely cared for, she'd have mentioned it to me. I would have when I was a young woman."

"Were there any other tenants in apartment four after the incident last year?" Stanley asked.

Mrs. Calvin shook her head. "It took time to clean the place up. I had it all redone. New paint, new flooring, new blinds and curtains. I didn't want to see anything that reminded me of how it was before. Katie moved in shortly after it was done. I guess it'll all have to be redone again." She blotted her eyes once more. "I liked Katie. She didn't deserve this."

Cooper squeezed her hand. "I know. I'm sorry."

He meant it too. He was sorry this had happened to her again. Sorry this had happened to both Katie Myers and Jill Kinner. Sorry he hadn't been able to stop the first murder or somehow foresee the second. Sorry for everything.

"Anything else you can tell us?" Stanley asked, still taking notes. "Do you have a family contact for her? A work contact? Anything?"

Mrs. Calvin nodded and got out of her chair. "I'll make you a copy of her rental agreement and application. That's all I can tell you, other than that she never gave me a bit of trouble."

She started crying in earnest as she went over to the filing cabinet that was in the small laundry area at the rear of the kitchen. She found the papers, ran them through the small copier that was set up on top of the filing cabinet, and handed the copies to Stanley.

"It's not worth it anymore," Mrs. Calvin said, sitting again. "I'm glad I already sold the building. I'm too old for this."

The location was popular with trendy young professionals. She had probably made good money here, but Cooper could certainly understand why she wanted to get out.

"You did the right thing," he said. "Take your money and retire in style."

That coaxed a grin from her. "I've got nothing to complain about. The buyer made me a good offer. They're supposed to start tearing the building up as soon as I move into a hotel."

Cooper whistled. "I hope they're paying for that too."

"You know it. And they're moving all my things into storage for me. I figured it was a nice reason to retire."

"I agree," Cooper told her. "You deserve that after everything you've been through in the last year."

"Anything else about the case?" Stanley asked, then drained his coffee cup.

Mrs. Calvin shook her head.

"If you think of anything or something comes up, please get in touch," Stanley said. He handed her a business card.

"I will," she said.

"Can we reach you at the hotel if we have any further questions?" Cooper asked.

"Of course," Mrs. Calvin answered. She gave him the name and address of the hotel and her room number.

"Thanks," Cooper said, jotting down the information in his notebook. The men stood up.

"Thanks for your help, ma'am," Cooper said. "I'm sorry about all this. I realize it's not easy."

Mrs. Calvin studied him. "Are you okay now? I mean . . ." She tapped the side of her head.

In spite of himself, Cooper cracked a slight smile. "That's been a matter of opinion since before I got shot, but the doctors say I'm fine physically."

She laughed, and then her expression softened. "You take care. I don't want to hear you're back at the hospital."

"No, I don't have any plans for that," Cooper responded.

"We're going to go upstairs," Stanley said. "See what the other officers have found. You'll have to stay clear of the apartment until we give you the okay."

Mrs. Calvin nodded. "I remember from last time. When your men are through, I'll make sure it stays locked up."

"Thank you," Stanley said, then gestured to Cooper. "Come on."

The two men went back up the stairs. By the time they walked into the apartment, the victim's body had been removed. There was only a tape outline where she had been. The bloodstains were still untouched. They would stay untouched until everything had been properly documented.

Kent hurried over to them. "It wasn't a robbery. Not from anything we can see so far. Her jewelry box has some pretty nice pieces in it. Her watch was an expensive model, still on her wrist. She's got a decent amount of cash and a stack of credit cards in her purse. None of it was touched."

"Anything else?" Stanley asked.

"Apparently no one saw the murderer enter the apartment," Kent said. "And it looks like all he did was kill her. Though that was more than enough as far as I'm concerned."

Once Cooper had heard everything the police knew, he paced around the apartment. He didn't concentrate on the blood or the broken lamp or the overturned chairs. Instead, he tried to see what he could deduce about this young woman whose life had so abruptly ended.

Katie had already packed most of her belongings. Judging from the boxes stacked in the bedroom, she had started packing in there. Cooper scanned the bookshelves that flanked the living room fireplace and noticed some medical books, a few classics, a volume of Shakespeare, and several popular novels.

He studied the pictures on the shelves. A young woman in a cap and gown smiling between proud parents. The same young woman in a fuchsia gown standing with three others identically dressed next to a beaming bride. A faded photo of a girl of ten or twelve with a slightly older boy and two younger ones at a water park. One of a tabby cat asleep on the same couch that was still in the room.

The frame on that one said *Lizzie*, and he wondered what had happened to the cat. The couch seemed fairly new. Katie had probably bought it when she moved in here less than a year ago. Did she still have the cat? If so, where was she?

As Cooper bent down to study the picture, he noticed the slightest movement in the bottom shelf. He dropped to one knee. The bottom shelf was full of books except for a large vase at one end. It was tall and rather narrow except for its wide base. Evidently, it was being used as a bookend. He smiled when he saw a pair of green eyes staring back at him from the darkness behind it.

"Come on, Lizzie," he said softly. He reached toward her.

With a growl, the cat tried to dash past him and escape.

Cooper caught her before she could get away, holding her against the carpet with both hands so she couldn't twist away from him or scratch. "You're safe. I won't hurt you."

Lizzie growled again, then emitted a plaintive cry.

"It's okay." He waved down Officer Kent. "Do you have a towel or something?"

Kent frowned at him. But he went over to one of the forensics guys and borrowed an empty canvas duffel bag. "Good luck," he said, setting the bag on the floor next to Cooper and the struggling cat.

Still using one hand to keep the cat down, Cooper placed the bag on top of her and then rolled her up in it.

Lizzie squirmed and hissed, but she couldn't get away.

"You're fine," he soothed, carefully stroking her behind the ears.

She growled again, trying to twist her head so she could snap at him, but he kept his hold and she finally calmed. A little anyway.

Cooper got to his feet, cradling the cat firmly against his chest.

Her eyes were wide and terrified, but she wasn't trying to escape anymore.

"That's it. Come on." He carried Lizzie over to Daniels and Kent. "What about the cat? She was hiding in the bookshelf."

"Forensics is done in the bathroom," Daniels said. "You can put her in there. She's got her litter box and food and water. Somebody will take her to a shelter before we leave."

Cooper glanced down at the cat in his arms. Lizzie was clearly an adult, but she was a little thing all the same, with tiny paws and delicate features. She had witnessed the horrific murder of her only friend, and she was supposed to be stored in a bathroom until someone came to take her to be put in a cage? He couldn't let it happen. "Could I take care of her until somebody in the victim's family claims her?"

Daniels thought for a minute. "You got what she needs?"

"No, but I can take what's here," Cooper said. "That should last a few days."

Daniels turned to Kent. "Hey, rookie. You're up on the latest. Any reason he can't do that?"

Kent shrugged. "I don't remember anything like that coming up. You can check with the captain."

"Sure thing," Cooper said. "When I get around to it." He walked over to Stanley. "You got anything yet?"

"Nothing but the obvious. Anything in here seem familiar to you?"

"I got nothing."

Cooper took the cat into the bathroom, closed the door, and let her go. He emptied the litter box into the trash can, then took the box along with fresh litter and cat food out to his car. Last of all, he apologized to Lizzie as he put her into the duffel bag. He pulled the string tight and carried her down to the car too. She wouldn't like it, but she'd be safe enough in there until he could get her home and set her up in his bathroom temporarily.

After that, Cooper planned to go see Jayla. She had dispatched the officers here, so she was aware of the situation. She knew someone else had been killed in apartment four, and it couldn't be easy for her to deal with. He needed to know how she was coping. And he wanted to see if she had remembered anything else from the incident last year when Jill Kinner had called 911 and talked to Jayla before she'd been murdered.

Cooper always felt a twinge of regret when he remembered telling Jayla that it was best if he didn't see her anymore. She had never tried to contact him after they'd broken up last year. Would she want to see him?

He needed to tell her that he wasn't going to let anything happen to her. But then again, he had no right to tell her that. Dane Wolff was in jail. He'd been in jail since last year, awaiting trial. He couldn't have been the one who killed Katie Myers tonight.

He winced as a horrible thought popped into his head. Had Cooper identified the wrong man as Jill Kinner's murderer? Was that why there had been a second victim? It was clear that he'd been correct to quit the force and distance himself from Jayla. Obviously, he couldn't protect her. He couldn't protect anyone.

But Cooper wasn't about to let Jayla go through this ordeal alone. Not after the nightmare she'd had to cope with a year ago.

Jayla hurried to her car, her keys clutched tightly in her hand, the largest one sticking out between her first and second fingers, a ready weapon if she needed one. She was used to working late, and it didn't usually bother her. But tonight she felt a horrible sense of dread.

She chided herself for not asking one of the officers on duty to walk her to her car. She knew any one of them would have gladly accompanied her.

Jayla quickened her stride, glancing around in case someone was hiding in the shadows. When her green Toyota was only a few feet away, she pressed the button on her key fob and heard the click of the lock. Finally, she made it to the car and peered into the back seat to make sure no one was hiding there before she opened the door. She almost dropped her keys when her phone buzzed. She slid into her seat, then shut the door and locked it.

After digging her phone out of her purse, Jayla caught a startled breath when she saw the name on the screen. She waited one more ring, steadying herself, and answered.

"Hey," Cooper said. His low, smooth voice always reminded her of black velvet, with a hint of a gravelly drawl.

She moistened her suddenly dry lips. "Did you already hear?"

"I did," he said.

From the background noise, Jayla could tell that he was driving. "Where are you?"

"Leaving the apartment house," Cooper answered. "Stanley let me come up to find out if I saw anything that would tie this murder to the one last year." He sighed. "I didn't notice anything."

Jayla was already sweating. She twisted the key in the ignition and cranked up the air-conditioning. "How did you find out about it so quickly?"

"I heard the call," Cooper said. "I've been listening to the scanner, and I've heard you a lot these past few months ever since you started working dispatch."

She was surprised that he'd been listening. Had it been for business reasons? Or had it been because he missed her? No, she wouldn't think about that. Things were over between them. Even though she didn't want to know the answer, she asked, "Why?"

"I listen to the scanner to keep up with what's going on in the area, in case I hear anything regarding something I'm working on," he explained. "I was headed out to hear Brandon play, but when I heard you give the address on the radio and mention apartment four, I had to go there."

Her stomach clenched. Jayla didn't want to think about that apartment. She didn't want to know about it.

"I had to call you," Cooper continued. "I knew you couldn't have a personal conversation while you were on duty, but I figured you were probably off by now. I thought maybe we could talk. I know you probably didn't want to hear from me ever again, but—"

"You were the one who ended things, remember?" Jayla interrupted. Her tone was sharper than she had intended it to be, but it was the truth.

"I thought you understood why," he said, his voice lower than before.

"I did," Jayla said, "but that doesn't mean I agreed."

"Can we talk for a little while?" Cooper asked. "I'll buy you a cup of coffee. What do you think?"

Jayla told herself that she didn't want to see him again. She didn't want to care about what happened to him or what he'd been doing in the eight months since their breakup. She should do what all her friends had told her and put him completely out of her mind.

But after what had happened earlier tonight, she needed to see him. Suddenly she wanted to talk to him about the murders, what they'd both been through because of what had happened in apartment four, and why he had told her goodbye.

Last year after Jill had been killed, Jayla had gone to the hospital every day to see Cooper while he was recovering from his injuries. He had become more and more distant with her, and he'd refused to talk about anything, including the murder, how he was feeling, and even their relationship. That had hurt.

It still did.

Jayla had pulled his doctor aside and asked if Cooper's injuries could have changed his personality. The doctor had agreed that it was possible and advised her to give him time to heal and cope with everything that had happened.

She had taken the doctor's advice. Jayla's visits had become less frequent. When Cooper had claimed he was tired, she had left his room. But she had seen the truth in his eyes. It was an excuse, and he didn't want her there. Jayla had tried to be patient with Cooper when he was in the hospital, when he was in rehab, and when he was finally cleared to work again.

She'd been patient until he'd announced that he was quitting the force. "You're what?" she'd asked, bewildered. "You can't quit just like that. At least get another job before you leave the department. What are you going to live on?"

"I've told you before that I wanted to go into business for myself," Cooper had said.

"Yes, and I think you'll be a wonderful private investigator someday," Jayla had replied. "But you can't start up day one making enough money to support yourself. That's crazy."

"I've been with the police for six years," he'd reminded her. "I've learned a lot in that time. And I know a PI who says I can apprentice with him until I'm ready to get out on my own. He's got more business than he can handle. That will get me started."

"Instead of quitting, couldn't you take a leave of absence?" she'd asked. "I'm sure the department would understand after what you've been through. I know it's hard to think about going back into the same kind of work that nearly got you killed, but you've barely started to recover. Give yourself some time before you make such a drastic decision about your career."

"The decision is already made," Cooper had said, and the coldness in his voice had felt like a blow.

It had been difficult to search his face and not see the love she was so used to seeing there. Finally, she'd whispered, "Are you sure?"

"This is something I have to do while I still can." His hard expression hadn't changed. "I can't spend my whole life waiting until everything is perfect before I try. I have to go ahead and do it."

"But what about us?"

"I have to get myself together," he'd told her. "What happened in that apartment . . . I have to figure things out all over again. What I'm supposed to do with my life and why I didn't die. And I have to do that on my own."

"You're breaking up with me," Jayla had said, and it wasn't a question. It was merely a sad confirmation.

"I'm letting you go. For your own good."

She had blinked hard, determined not to cry, then lifted her chin. "Will you keep me posted on how you're doing?"

"No. I don't want to hurt you," Cooper had said. "I think it's best for both of us if we leave things here."

Jayla had taken a deep breath and then let it out very slowly. "I hope you find what you really want." Without another word, she had walked away.

Was Jayla supposed to walk back to him just because there had been another murder in the same apartment? Or was he simply trying to soothe his conscience about the way things had ended between them?

She wasn't sure at this point, but there was nobody else who could understand what she was feeling right now. Nobody but him.

Jayla finally suggested a café, wondering how long she'd been lost in her thoughts.

Cooper chuckled softly. "That's what I was thinking."

It was the same restaurant they used to frequent together. When they were on duty at all hours, they needed someplace that was open 24-7. The café was located a few blocks from the police station.

"Are you on your way?" she asked.

"Not quite yet," he said, suddenly sounding uncomfortable. "I have to take care of something first. Thirty minutes?"

Jayla didn't want to sit alone in a restaurant at this time of night, but she could drive around until it was time to meet him. "Sure."

"Great. See you then."

She considered what Cooper had to take care of so late. Maybe he was on a date. But that didn't make sense. He wouldn't take a date to a crime scene. She remembered that he'd been going to a jazz club when he'd heard the call. Perhaps he'd been on the way to meet someone there.

Jayla shook her head. It didn't matter. Their relationship was over, and the sole reason they were even meeting for coffee was to figure out how the murder tonight was tied to the one last year. *If* it was.

She drove around for twenty-five minutes before parking in front of the bold mural painted on the side of the café. Something about the vibrant colors and bright lights made her feel a bit more normal. She wasn't new to the graveyard shift. She wasn't easy to rattle. At least she hadn't been until a year ago.

Setting her jaw, Jayla exited her car and went inside. As always, the café was as noisy and full as if it were seven or eight in the evening rather than the middle of the night. Most of the patrons had come from the local clubs, many of those from their regular jobs as musicians, sound techs, and bouncers.

She scanned the restaurant and saw Cooper sitting at the little square table in the corner. Their table. She walked over to him.

"I'm glad you came." He stood and pulled out a chair for her.

"Thanks," Jayla said, sitting down. He was always a gentleman, something she'd seen far too seldom since their breakup, something she missed.

"I ordered coffee for both of us," Cooper said as he sat across from her. "I hope that's okay."

She nodded.

"I figured you'd be thinking about last year, and I wanted to make sure you were doing well. I realize it was bad for you."

"I wasn't the one who was shot in the head."

He touched the dark hair over his temple, then shook his head slightly. "I wasn't the one who had to listen to a woman being murdered."

Jayla shuddered as the memory of that night returned to her. "I'm fine," she said, and it was mostly true. "What about you?"

"Doing okay. I moved a little farther out of the neighborhood."

"Oh? Where to?"

"On the other side of the arena."

She smiled. He hadn't changed that much. "You still like your hockey," she accused playfully.

"I'll bet you do too," Cooper countered.

Jayla grinned. "Go Stars."

She had learned to love the game as she'd learned to love him. She wasn't sure if it was comforting or painful to watch without him. Maybe a bit of both, though she rarely went to the games anymore. It wasn't the same without him.

She knew he hadn't invited her here to talk about hockey, so she asked, "What did you discover tonight?"

The waitress brought their cups of coffee before Cooper could answer.

After the waitress left, he poured cream into his cup as he'd always done and took a sip. "Not much yet. Same apartment. Same MO. This time nobody saw the shooter."

"And the victim?" She knew it was foolish to hope, but she couldn't help it.

"Katie Myers is dead. I'm sorry."

"Me too." Jayla sipped her coffee, grimaced, and added the sugar she'd forgotten. "Could it be the same guy?"

"Not if Wolff was the killer the first time," Cooper replied. "That's why I wanted to talk to you. And that's why I wanted to make sure you're all right." He sighed. "If Wolff is innocent like he's been saying all this time, then I botched things worse than I already thought."

"But you saw him."

"I thought I did," he said, raking a hand through his hair. "But . . ."

Jayla raised her eyebrows. "Now you think you were wrong?"

"What else could explain it? Someone else in that apartment is dead, so I must have identified the wrong man."

"You told the truth," she said. "You reported what you saw."

"What I believed I saw," Cooper said. "I got there too late to save Jill Kinner. And because I made a mistake last year, Katie Myers is dead as well. If I'd done my job, the real killer wouldn't have been free to kill again."

"You don't know that for sure," Jayla said firmly. "This could be a copycat."

"Yeah, I suppose. Or I could have been wrong when I thought it was Wolff. His attorneys have made a lot of noise about me having a head injury. They're going to try to tear me apart with that at the trial."

"That's not your problem. Your job is to tell the truth about what you saw. The rest is up to the jury."

"What if Wolff really is innocent?"

She cringed. The anguish in his eyes nearly broke her heart. "Do you believe he is?"

"I saw him." Cooper rubbed his forehead. "I know I saw him."

Unable to stop herself, Jayla reached over and took his hand. "Do you still have headaches?"

He put his free hand over hers, a touch of warmth and wistfulness in his smile. "No, not anymore."

"Good. I'm glad." She pulled her hand away before she began imagining that things could be any different than they were. "So what happens now? With the case, I mean."

Cooper shrugged. "Same as usual, I guess. Stanley and his men will finish their investigation at the scene, forensics will analyze what they find, and they'll try to figure out who is responsible. I suppose they'll make sure Wolff was where he's supposed to be."

"He never made bail, did he?"

"No bail after he and his wife were caught at the airport with passports that weren't theirs."

Jayla shook her head, recalling the media frenzy when Dane Wolff and his wife, Laurel, had been caught at the airport trying to board a plane to Brazil, but they'd said it was all a mistake. They'd claimed that they were taking a relaxing vacation, and they'd misunderstood the terms of Dane's release. The couple had insisted that they had no idea the passports weren't theirs. They belonged to their employees, and they'd gotten mixed up with their own important documents.

"I don't understand why his wife has stayed with him all this time," she said. "Especially if he was seeing Jill on the side."

"I don't know," Cooper responded. "But Laurel always claimed he was innocent."

"Laurel was her husband's alibi," Jayla said. "She said he was with her the entire night."

He nodded. "And she said that she knew about Jill. That the affair had ended before the murder and that she had forgiven her husband. Both of them insist Jill was killed by someone else, maybe the maintenance man at the apartment."

"Did they check him out?"

"Yeah, but they didn't discover anything to tie him to the murder." Cooper drained his cup and pushed it toward the edge of the table, signaling to their waitress that he was ready for a refill. "Can I ask you something?"

"I suppose," she said hesitantly. She watched him closely, knowing from the tone of his voice that he was going to bring up something difficult.

"I wouldn't normally ask, because you don't like to talk about it," he said, "but this whole thing has already been torn wide open tonight."

"I realize that," Jayla murmured.

"I have a feeling Stanley or one of his people will ask you about it anyway in the next day or two."

"You want to know if I've remembered anything else from last year." She stared into her coffee cup, hearing again the worst parts of that 911 call, feeling her stomach pitch and roil.

"Are you okay?"

For a moment he sounded strange and far away. Jayla gazed at him, her small smile tight. "Why couldn't you meet me immediately when you called me tonight?"

Cooper seemed surprised by the question. "I had to drop somebody off at my house. I didn't want her to wait out in the car. It's too hot."

Of course there would be another woman. Still, he'd never been the type to take one home with him. It went against what they both believed. "I see," she said, trying to sound disinterested. "And how was the club? How's Brandon?"

"Never got to see him," he said. "I heard that call about the apartment and headed straight over there."

"With your date?"

"She wasn't my date," Cooper said, a gleam of humor in his eyes.

Jayla frowned. "No?"

"I picked her up at the scene."

Her frown deepened. He was picking up women at murder scenes now?

"Her name is Lizzie," he continued. "She has the most beautiful green eyes you ever saw."

Jayla felt her blood heat at the smugness in his expression. When had he become so insensitive? She shoved away from the table and stood. "You could at least keep that sort of thing to yourself when you're talking to me."

"Come on," Cooper said. "You don't—"

She spun on her heel and marched toward the door.

"Wait a minute," he called after her.

Jayla didn't stop. She heard him say something to the waitress, but she was too mad to care. She was almost to her car when he caught up to her.

"At least hear me out," Cooper insisted.

She whirled around and glared at him, waiting for an explanation.

"Please come back and finish your coffee," he said. "I'd like to explain to you about Lizzie."

Jayla crossed her arms over her chest. "The Lizzie who's waiting for you at your house?"

"I'm not sure how long she'll be staying," Cooper said. "Until somebody comes to get her, I guess."

"Comes to get her?" Jayla repeated, completely baffled. "Just who—"

"How much do you know about taking care of a cat?"

She gaped at him, then laughed. "Lizzie's a cat? You're such a jerk." She gave him a playful shove.

"I know," he said, taking her hand and ushering her toward the café, "but I made you laugh."

"You did. How did you get a cat?"

His smile vanished. "She belonged to Katie Myers. They were going to take her to a shelter, but I figured the poor thing had been through enough already. I'm keeping her until somebody in Katie's family claims her."

"That's sweet of you." Jayla squeezed his hand. He was always sweet. "I'm sorry I got mad."

"I'm sorry I teased you," Cooper said. "You used to like it when I joked around."

She shook her head ruefully. "My best friend in grade school had an older brother who used to pester her all the time. I think the two of you would have been best friends."

He didn't deny it. Instead, he laughed that low, easy way she remembered so well.

They returned to their table. Evidently he had asked the waitress to keep it for them, because nothing had been touched. They sat down, and abruptly he was sober. She knew he was going to ask about that night again.

"I'm sorry, but I need to know," Cooper began. "Tell me everything you remember about what happened a year ago."

Jayla felt a sinking in the pit of her stomach. "All I remember about last time is how horrible it was. I've blocked out the rest, and I don't want to revisit it."

"Okay," he said gently. "I don't want to make this any worse for you."

"I'm sorry," she told him. "I'm aware this is important for a lot of reasons."

"Don't worry about it," Cooper assured her. "Stanley will get to the bottom of it."

They made small talk as they lingered over their coffee. Jayla couldn't believe that she was sitting across from Cooper. It felt unreal, like everything else that had happened during the last few hours.

As Cooper walked Jayla to her car, he averted his gaze. "Can I ask you for a favor?"

She took a steadying breath. "Sure."

"If anything comes up about the case, can I call you and see if it reminds you of anything?"

"If you want to," Jayla said. "I'll try, but I can't swear I'll remember."

"I understand," Cooper said. He sounded disappointed. "Last year messed us both up pretty bad, didn't it? I figure the only way we're going to get over it and move on is if we find out what actually happened to both victims and why. I need your help."

"I'll do everything I can," she promised.

But she had a terrible feeling that her best wouldn't be nearly enough.

Cooper loosened his tie and turned the fan up a notch. Even with the blinds closed, the heat poured through the west-facing window in his tiny office. Dallas office space was at a premium, so he put up with the heat as best he could. He wasn't in here very often anyway. There wasn't much a private investigator could do from the confines of his office.

He was getting ready to drive over to the apartment, hoping Stanley would know more about the murder of Katie Myers, when there was a quiet knock on his door.

A tall, elegant woman with red-lacquered nails and platinum hair entered the room. She pushed her sunglasses to the top of her head, revealing eyes so dark they were nearly black. "Are you Cooper Cole?" Her voice was low and silky, but there was nothing unbusinesslike about it.

"Yes I am," he said, standing up. "How may I help you?"

She glanced over her shoulder, then shut the door. "I'd like to hire you for a case."

"Please have a seat," Cooper said, gesturing to the chair on the other side of the desk. "May I get you something to drink? Coffee? Water?"

"No thank you." She took the chair he offered. Despite the heat, she appeared as cool as ice in her white linen pantsuit. "You don't know me, but I know you. At least, I know of you."

He sat down and waited for her to go on.

"I'm Laurel Wolff."

Cooper nodded. He should have recognized her, even though he hadn't met her before. Laurel was the wife of entrepreneur Dane Wolff, notable in her own right for her charity work in the community.

"If you've come to talk to me about changing my testimony, then you shouldn't have bothered," he said.

"My husband's attorneys informed me that they've been in contact with you a number of times in the past year regarding your testimony," Laurel said. "Clearly, you must know that you were mistaken about what you saw when that woman was killed last year."

"I can't discuss this with you," Cooper responded. He felt for the woman. It couldn't be easy to be married to a man who'd been accused of murdering the woman he'd cheated on her with. But he couldn't compromise his integrity. Jill Kinner deserved justice.

"I understand you had a head wound at the time, and you struggled with a difficult recovery," she continued as if he hadn't spoken. "And, yes, I'm aware that my husband was renting the apartment. It's only natural that he would be the first one to be suspected in the woman's murder. However, after what happened last night, it's obvious that you were wrong."

"I told the police what I saw," he insisted. "The murder last night could very well be a copycat, someone with a fascination for killing and notoriety."

"But you must admit that last night's murder couldn't have been committed by Dane," Laurel reasoned. "He's still in jail. I visited him this morning and told him what happened."

"No, you're absolutely right. Unless he had some extraordinary means of getting out of jail and then back in again, he couldn't have done it."

"Then—"

"But that doesn't clear him of Jill Kinner's murder," Cooper interrupted. "The one last night has no bearing on the other."

"But it does," she insisted. "He's innocent. If he couldn't have killed the woman last night and she was killed exactly like the first one, then doesn't that at least raise more questions? The evidence against Dane deserves a second look."

He couldn't deny that he'd had the same thought, even though he had been a witness at the scene of the first murder. "Is it possible that your husband was at the scene? Either during or after the murder? That maybe I saw him leave even if he wasn't the killer?"

"No. Like I told the police, he was with me the entire night. We were at home together. They found nothing on his clothes or in his car—no evidence whatsoever—that linked him to the crime scene."

"Except that he was the one leasing the apartment," Cooper reminded her. "His prints were everywhere, and he doesn't deny having an affair with Jill."

Laurel crossed her arms over her chest. "Neither of us ever claimed he didn't know that woman or that he hadn't been seeing her. But their relationship was over. I forgave him. We'd been—" She glanced down, and her thick lashes swept against her cheeks. "I hadn't been treating him very well."

"What do you mean?"

"We've been trying to have children since we were married fourteen years ago. He wanted to adopt, but I wouldn't consider it. I was mad at him for even suggesting it." Laurel sighed. "I know it wasn't his fault. It wasn't mine either. It's just the way it is. How could I blame him for wanting to spend time with someone who didn't treat him like a failure?"

Cooper said nothing. Maybe he didn't understand everything about the murder of Jill Kinner. Getting shot in the head could have affected his memory and made him suggestible. It was possible that last night's murder had occurred because he had identified the wrong man, leaving the real killer free to kill again.

"Why are you telling me this?" he asked, unable to admit what he was considering. "This is something you should be discussing with the police or your husband's lawyers or the DA."

"I've already talked to all of them," she replied. "Well, I left a message for the DA, asking him to meet with me and my husband's attorneys. I called Officer Stanley about last night's murder, but he said they're still investigating and he couldn't tell me anything."

"They can't yet," Cooper confirmed. "Give them time. But they can help you a lot more than I can. I'm not even on the force anymore."

"I understand you can't reopen the investigation or anything like that," Laurel said. "But if you can produce evidence that would implicate someone besides my husband, then the DA would have no choice but to stop the trial before it's too late."

The trial was scheduled for May 18. The date was etched into his brain. He was the lone eyewitness to Wolff's presence at the apartment at the time of the murder. Was Cooper remembering that night correctly? He'd been so sure all these months. He could still see Wolff's face, his eyes wild as he burst from the apartment door with the number four on it, gun in hand. But it was only a glimpse before everything was enveloped in darkness and pain.

"Why are you asking me to investigate?" he asked. "I was a witness in the first murder."

"That's why I want you to do it. You're already familiar with the case."

"Do you have anyone in particular in mind who might have murdered Jill?"

"Daryl Peters, the maintenance man at the apartment building," she answered without hesitation. "The police hardly talked to him after they arrested my husband."

"Why would the maintenance man murder Jill?" Cooper asked.

"I don't know. Jealousy? Maybe he'd been rejected by her. He might have killed her because she was seeing Dane and not him."

"You said Dane and Jill's relationship was over," he reminded her.

"It was. We were working on our marriage. Dane told her they were through, and she had to move out of the apartment when the lease was up."

"When would that have been?"

"The end of June. Dane thought that almost two months would be a reasonable amount of time for her to get a new place."

"I guess that seems fair enough," he said. "I never heard what she did for a living."

Her dark eyes flashed. "Leeched off my husband."

Cooper watched her patiently, waiting for an explanation.

"She was a flight attendant, but she quit when Dane moved her into that apartment." Laurel bit her lower lip. "She might have gone back to that after Dane left her."

He thought about Mrs. Calvin, the landlady at the apartment building. She'd visited from time to time with Katie over the past few months. She might have conversations with her other tenants. Maybe Jill had chatted with her too. It was possible that she'd confided in Mrs. Calvin. He made a mental note to find out.

"Wasn't Daryl Peters questioned in the original investigation?" he asked.

"Yes, but the police are sure they have the killer. Why would they bother searching for anybody else?"

Cooper wanted to argue, but he knew things like that happened. The department was already stretched as thin as it could be. Officers were overworked and underpaid. They had enough work to do without adding more, especially the kind that never panned out. Unless, of course, it did pan out once someone actually took the trouble to do it.

He took a deep breath. "I'll see what I can learn." He would look into the case, but he was never going to risk his life—or anyone else's—ever again.

"Thank you so much," Laurel said. "I knew I could count on you to do the right thing."

Cooper nodded, but a sense of trepidation suddenly enveloped him. What would he uncover during his search?

He hoped he hadn't made a tragic mistake.

Cooper spent the weekend reviewing both murder cases and getting Lizzie used to her new home. Temporary home, he reminded himself frequently, but he decided it was far too soon to bother Katie's family about taking the cat. They had enough to deal with as it was.

He was relieved that Lizzie had a healthy appetite and seemed to be doing fine. But she still hid under the bed most of the time and liked to tear up toilet paper when Cooper wasn't home. It surprised him how much he was starting to like having the cat around. Somehow she was a comforting presence, even when she was hiding or causing mischief.

It wasn't until the Monday after the murder that anything significant came up. Stanley had told him that they'd arrested Daryl Peters, the maintenance man at the apartment building. Cooper decided to try once more to talk to Jayla. Her phone rang three times before she answered.

Cooper frowned. It sounded like Jayla's voice, but it was slightly different. "Is this Mary Ann?"

Mary Ann was Jayla's younger sister. She'd moved into Jayla's place after the murder last year. Jayla claimed it was because Mary Ann was ready to leave their parents' house, but Cooper had a feeling that it was more because Jayla didn't feel comfortable living alone anymore. He didn't blame her. Especially since he'd broken things off with her not long after the killing.

"Yes," she said. "What do you want?"

"It's Cooper Cole."

"Yeah, I know." Mary Ann sounded more than a little protective and angry. It was obvious that she hadn't forgiven him for hurting her sister.

"Is Jayla there?" he asked.

"She's off duty today, so she slept late. She's getting dressed, and she asked me to answer her phone."

"Would you please tell her to call me when she gets a minute?" Cooper asked. "It's kind of important."

"Is it about that new murder or something else?" she asked.

"Please ask her to call me. She can tell you about it later if she wants to."

"I guess I could do that," Mary Ann said with only faint reluctance. "I'll tell her to—"

"Is that Cooper?" Jayla asked in the background. "Give me the phone."

Mary Ann huffed.

"Hi," Jayla said. She sounded slightly breathless.

He wondered if she had rushed across the room or if she was nervous about the topic of his call. "How are you?" he asked, making his voice as soothing as he could. "I didn't mean to interrupt what you were doing."

"Oh, it's no problem," she replied. "It's my day off, and I wasn't busy. What's up?"

"I have some news about the case," Cooper said.

"I don't know anything about it besides dispatching a unit to the scene," Jayla said quickly. "I can't—"

"Wait. Please hear me out," Cooper said, cutting her off. He knew that everything about this case was tied to the one last year. He didn't want to think about that one any more than she did. But if he could find the killer to prevent future murders and keep an innocent man from being convicted, he couldn't simply ignore it. He didn't think she could either.

"All right," she said. "What is it?"

"Stanley told me that they've arrested a man named Daryl Peters. Have you ever heard of him?"

"No," Jayla said. "Who is he?"

"The maintenance man at the apartment house," he answered. "Stanley says he does work for several of the small apartment buildings in the area. I heard the name in connection with Jill's murder."

"Was he a suspect?"

"He was a person of interest, mostly because he didn't have much of an alibi at the time of the killing. He claimed he was home alone. But there was no physical evidence to connect him. And I had seen Wolff coming out of Jill's apartment. Or I thought I had."

"Are you still second-guessing yourself about that?" Jayla asked, a note of concern in her voice.

Cooper exhaled. "I don't know. Maybe. I think it wouldn't hurt to investigate some more to be completely sure."

"If that's what you need to do," she said, her voice a little stiff. "How you go about it isn't important to me."

"I was wondering if you'd help me out too."

"What do you want me to do?"

"I'm planning to talk to Peters," he said. "Will you go with me?"

"What?" Jayla gasped. "Why? I thought they didn't have anything on him."

"That was last time. It's more complicated this time."

"What do you mean?"

"Peters has deep scratches on his neck. The police are comparing his DNA to what was under Katie's fingernails when she died."

"Isn't that enough?" she asked. "Won't that prove or disprove that he was involved?"

"It's not always that easy," Cooper replied. "Peters insists that he didn't have anything to do with the killings either time."

"Isn't that what everyone who's been arrested for murder says?"

"Pretty much, yeah. But I want to talk to this guy and see what he has to say. Stanley said his explanation for those scratches is pretty far out there. I'd like to hear it firsthand."

"I think you're old enough to visit him on your own," Jayla remarked. "Where do I come in?"

"I was hoping you'd listen to his voice and see if there was anything familiar about it." Cooper braced himself, waiting for her reaction.

"No, you don't need me."

"I do need you. I'm sorry this is difficult for you, but I don't want you to do anything but listen to the guy talk for a minute or two. Then you can leave if you want. Is that too much to ask?"

She didn't respond.

"Anyone who's on the hook for either or both of these murders is in a world of trouble," Cooper continued. "Yes, I want whoever's behind this to be caught and punished, but only if he's actually guilty. Maybe you can clear this guy at least for the murder last year."

"But all I know about is the 911 call," Jayla reminded him, "and I've blocked out most of it."

"Peters won't connect you with the call," he said. "He'll think you're with me. All I want is a yes or no on the voice. Please?"

There was silence on the other end of the phone.

"I'm sorry," Cooper said at last. "I knew I shouldn't have asked. You've been through more than enough already."

"And so have you," Jayla said. "I understand why you're doing this. You need to make sure you saw what really happened and figure out if the two murders are related." She took a deep breath. "When are you planning to visit Peters?"

"As soon as possible."

She huffed. "If you're sure this is going to help, pick me up in twenty minutes."

"Great. Thank you. I promise you don't have to stay a minute longer than you feel comfortable with."

"Okay. I'll be waiting for you."

"See you soon." Cooper hung up the phone and stared at it, hoping he wasn't pulling Jayla into something that would hurt her more than he already had.

Cooper rang the doorbell at Jayla's house twenty minutes later.

Jayla answered the door. She was dressed casually in a T-shirt, jeans, and tennis shoes, and her tawny hair was pulled into a ponytail at the base of her neck. She looked as if she'd been in college last week instead of several years ago. All the same, there was a pinched wariness in her expression that made him wonder if this was a good idea.

She gave him a wry smile. "You're prompt as usual."

"I didn't want you to change your mind," he said.

Mary Ann walked over and scowled at Cooper. "I've been trying to talk her out of it. She's a dispatcher, not a police officer. This kind of thing isn't in her job description."

Mary Ann was the spitting image of her sister. She had the same light-brown hair, green eyes, and arched dark brows. But Mary Ann was a few years younger and not nearly as patient as Jayla.

Cooper offered her his most charming smile. "Good to see you again."

Mary Ann gave him the once-over. "I guess we never got a real goodbye, did we?"

"No, we didn't," he said. "Things weren't easy for any of us."

Mary Ann's features softened the slightest bit. "Maybe not." She touched her sister's arm. "Are you sure this is what you want to do?"

"I'll be okay," Jayla assured her. "I don't think we'll be gone long."

Mary Ann crossed her arms. "Call me if you need a ride home."

That made Jayla laugh. "I promise."

It wasn't a very long drive to the jail, and Cooper and Jayla spent the time catching up.

"How's Lizzie?" Jayla asked.

"She's settling in without too much trouble," he replied, "but she's reluctant to come out from under the bed. At least she's eating."

"When are you going to get in touch with the family about taking her?"

"Soon." Cooper grinned. "But I'm not in a big hurry. It's nice to have her around."

"It was good of you to take her," Jayla said, staring out the window. "Sometimes people forget that pets can be traumatized too."

"She was pretty scared when I found her in the apartment. With everything that was going on, I don't think anyone else even noticed her."

"Maybe when she's more settled, you can introduce us." She gave him a hopeful glance. "I mean, if you have her much longer."

"I'd like that. You've had cats, haven't you?"

Jayla seemed faintly surprised at the question. "When I was a kid. Why?"

"After we're done at the jail, I thought you could help me pick out some toys for her. I didn't take any from the apartment, so she must be pretty bored at my place with nothing to do."

She smiled. "Cats sleep most of the time anyway."

"And tear up toilet paper." Cooper chuckled. "Ask me how I know."

He could tell she was trying to keep from laughing, but she sobered as he went through the interchange. They were almost at the detention center.

"I don't want to push you into anything you're not ready for," he said quietly. "I'm serious. I understand how it is for you. I feel the same way about digging into this whole thing again. I wouldn't do it if it wasn't important to so many people."

Jayla studied him for a moment. "There's something you're not telling me."

Cooper figured that she had the right to know. "Laurel Wolff came to see me."

She raised her eyebrows. "Dane Wolff's wife?"

"Yes. She hired me to do some investigating for her."

"Why? I would think you'd be the last one she'd hire considering you were involved in the first murder and it was your eyewitness account that got her husband locked up."

"That's precisely why she wants me to investigate, because I'm already familiar with the case."

"You mean because she wants you to change your testimony before there's a trial," Jayla said, perceptive as ever.

"Could be," he admitted. "She says she wants me to check into some things about the Kinner murder that she thinks the police have passed over."

"Like what?"

"Who else could have been involved at the time."

"And why the police didn't really look into other suspects because they already had an eyewitness identification of Dane Wolff."

Cooper winced. "Yes, she did bring that up. If it wasn't for the other night, I would have told her it was ridiculous to even consider anyone else. But now I'm not so sure."

"How does Peters fit into all of this?" she asked.

"That's exactly what I want to find out."

The man sitting on the other side of the glass appeared to be in his late fifties. Daryl Peters was stocky with graying blond hair and desperate pale-blue eyes.

Cooper picked up the receiver and waited as Peters did the same on the other side.

Peters adjusted his thick glasses as he peered at Cooper and Jayla. "Who are you?"

"My name's Cooper Cole. I was the officer who responded to the 911 call at Mrs. Calvin's apartment house last year."

"Yeah, you were shot," Peters said. "And you identified the killer. I remember reading that." He shook his head. "I'm supposed to have my lawyer present if you're going to question me."

"No, this isn't anything like that," Cooper said. "I'm not on the force anymore. I'm a private investigator."

Peters motioned to Jayla. "What about her? Is she a PI too?"

Jayla took the phone from Cooper, but he leaned close so he could still hear the other side of the conversation.

"I'm a police dispatcher," she said. "I sent a unit over to Mrs. Calvin's Thursday night when Katie Myers was murdered. Nothing you say in front of me is official, okay?"

"All right," Peters said, but he didn't sound convinced. "What are you doing here?"

Jayla glanced at Cooper. "I'm helping him figure out what really happened and whether or not the two murders are connected."

"They're not connected by me," Peters protested. "All I know is that this whole thing is a setup."

Cooper took the receiver, still leaning close so Jayla could hear too. "Why don't you tell us what happened and why you were arrested?"

Peters pulled down the collar of his denim shirt, exposing three deep scratches on his neck. "When the police came to ask me what I knew about the young woman who was murdered, they saw these cuts and hauled me in."

"They claim Ms. Myers scratched you in an attempt to fight you off," Cooper said.

Peters nodded.

"What do you say?" Cooper asked.

"I tell you it's a setup," Peters replied. "Last Thursday afternoon, I was working in front of another apartment house near Mrs. Calvin's. Their regular lawn guy was on vacation, and I usually fill in for him. Anyhow, I'd finished mowing and was cleaning up around the sidewalk and the curb. It must have been almost a hundred degrees, and I couldn't wait to get out of there and back to my place for a cold drink."

"And?" Cooper prompted.

"Well, this woman in a long black coat came up to me," Peters continued. "I couldn't believe she was wearing a coat in the heat. Without a word, she scratched me down my neck and then took off around the corner. I was too shocked to do anything but watch her go. It was crazy."

Jayla leaned closer to the phone. "Did you know her?"

"Nobody I'd ever seen before," Peters said, touching the long red marks on his neck. "And I can't say I'd recognize her if I saw her again. She was there and gone so fast."

"What did she look like?" Cooper asked.

"She was white, tall for a woman, heavyset, and had long, dark hair."

"What time did this happen?" Cooper asked.

"About ten to fifteen minutes after four," Peters answered. "By the time I packed up my equipment and got home to clean the scratches, it was 4:25."

"That's a pretty wild story," Cooper admitted. "You really can't blame the police for being skeptical, can you?"

Peters slumped in his chair. "No, I guess not. But I swear every word is true."

"Did anyone see you at the time?" Jayla asked.

Peters shook his head. "Like I said, it was hot, so no one was out on the street. I wouldn't have been if I hadn't promised to get that yard done before the weekend."

"What about that night?" Cooper pressed. "Where were you when the murder was committed? It was around two o'clock in the morning."

"Where I was when the last one was committed," Peters said. "At home."

"Can anyone confirm that?" Cooper asked.

Peters shook his head, clearly miserable.

Jayla leaned close to the phone again. "You're the maintenance man for Mrs. Calvin's apartment house, right?"

"Yes," Peters said.

"Did you know both of the women who were killed?" she asked.

"I'd seen them around," Peters said. "I might have done a few minor repairs in that apartment. Probably helped them carry in packages or groceries or something. I've tried to think of something specific, but I can't come up with anything. Nothing major. And I doubt I would have recognized either of the young ladies if I had seen them out somewhere away from the apartment."

Cooper raised an eyebrow at Jayla, who shook her head. He took that to mean she was out of questions too, so he told the suspect, "You've been very helpful, and we appreciate you talking to us."

"Do you think you can do anything to get me out of this mess?" Peters asked. "I'm innocent."

"Don't you have a lawyer?" Cooper asked.

Peters sighed. "Court appointed. If he has time for me."

"You hang tight," Cooper said. "I'm going to see what I can find out as quickly as possible. Is there anything else I should be aware of?"

"One other thing," Peters said. "The woman who scratched me was wearing rubber gloves. With claws."

"**R**ubber gloves with claws?" Jayla asked as she and Cooper drove away from the detention facility. "I didn't expect Peters to say anything like that."

"I think I know what kind of gloves he was talking about," Cooper said. "There's a lady a couple of houses down from mine who has a pair. They're really weird, but they're supposed to help you dig in your garden. You can buy them online."

"That's so strange." She frowned. "Why do you think someone would use gloves to scratch him?"

"Maybe she didn't want anything in his blood somehow contaminating her," he suggested. "But I'm more concerned about why anybody would want to scratch him in the first place."

"Assuming he's telling the truth."

Cooper glanced over at Jayla. She was staring out the window. There wasn't much to see, and even if there was, she was born and raised out here. She would have seen it all a million times already. Was she trying to keep him from seeing her face?

He shouldn't have asked her to visit Peters in the first place. She had told him that she didn't want to come. He'd known before he'd asked that this was going to be unpleasant for her.

"I'm sorry," he said softly.

Jayla met his gaze, and there were tears in her eyes.

They were in front of the old red courthouse. It was a large Gothic stone building with turrets. Cooper and his brother had called it

Frankenstein's castle when they were growing up. It was a museum now. He pulled into the parking lot. By the time he stopped the car, she was staring out the window again.

"I'm sorry," Cooper said once more, wanting to wrap her in his arms and hold her close. "I shouldn't have asked you to do this. I thought maybe if you heard the guy, you'd be able to tell if—"

"No," she said, her voice thick with tears, and then she sniffled and started digging in her purse.

"Our visit with Peters isn't the only thing that's bothering you, is it?" he asked. "You've been upset since Katie Myers was killed."

Jayla shrank away from him slightly. "I haven't been sleeping well."

"You should have told me. I would never have asked—"

"No, it's all right." She removed a tissue from her purse, then blotted her cheeks. "I'm not that fragile. Truly I'm not. Or at least I didn't used to be."

Cooper reached over and took her hand. "I know how awful that first murder was for you."

"I was a 911 operator," Jayla said. "I heard terrible things in some of those calls, but the one last year was worse than I can ever explain. It was like listening to pure evil. He took pleasure in her pain and terror. He enjoyed her suffering. And listening to it all—" She ducked her head and blotted her eyes again.

"It was like it was happening to you," he said gently. "I'm so sorry."

She pressed her lips together and sat up straighter. "I heard Jill drop the phone when he entered the apartment. Later the investigators found her phone under an end table. Maybe if he'd known I was on the line, he would have left without doing anything to her. I should have shouted or something, let him know she wasn't alone."

"Maybe he wouldn't have cared," Cooper said. "He told her that he was going to kill her, didn't he?"

Jayla nodded.

"I didn't get there fast enough." *To save her or you.*

She sighed. "It wasn't your fault. You got there as fast as you possibly could. There aren't enough officers to be everywhere at once." She smiled. "We both tried our best. It simply wasn't enough that time."

"Yeah, but in the kind of jobs we were doing, not succeeding can have some pretty serious consequences." He gave her a rueful grin. "Anyway, I shouldn't have dragged you into this. I suppose you would have told me if you'd recognized Peters's voice."

"I've been trying," she said, her voice taut and thin. "I've been forcing myself to go back over everything I can remember from that call. There's not much there anymore. A few parts have popped up when I least expect them. The vivid parts that I still can't seem to shake no matter how hard I try to make them go away. And, yes, I can still hear his voice, but it wasn't a normal voice."

"What do you mean?" Cooper asked.

Jayla squeezed her eyes shut. "His voice was low and deep, somewhere between a growl and a hiss, something you'd imagine a demon sounding like. It was almost inhuman, and the more terrible the things he said were, the more demonic his voice was. It didn't sound like Peters, but it didn't sound like anybody I've ever heard before or since."

"Don't think about it anymore. Please don't think about it ever again." He reached over and pulled her as close as the console between the two seats would allow. "I should never have asked you about it. This is my problem, not yours."

She gazed at him and cupped his face with her hand. "You were always so sweet. It's all right." She pulled away from him. "Really it is. I can handle it."

"I know you can. I'm glad your sister is staying with you anyway."

"Mary Ann thinks you're a jerk," Jayla said with an unsteady grin.

"I can tell," Cooper said. "Then she should be glad that we're not together anymore."

"She is."

He shook his head as he put the car back into gear and started driving again.

"She doesn't mean it," Jayla said. "She liked you a lot, and she wanted us to end up together."

"So did I," Cooper admitted, keeping his eyes on the road.

She remained silent for a few moments. Then she said, "You don't have to explain again. I know."

There were so many things that he wanted to tell Jayla. Instead, he remained silent as he drove her home.

When they arrived at her house, he escorted her to the front door and left with a quick goodbye.

Cooper returned to his car and checked his watch. His younger brother lived in the area, and he was probably off duty by now. It would be a good time to catch up with Kelly and find out if he'd heard any news about the murder. He was a police officer at the same station where Cooper used to work.

Cooper drove away from Jayla's house. "Call Kelly," he said aloud.

Kelly's voice came through the car speakers. "Hey, what's up?"

"I'm out your way. Mind if I stop by?"

"If you don't mind the place being a mess," Kelly replied. "Jen's working, and I just got home from work."

"No big deal," Cooper said.

"But don't tell Jen. She likes people to think everything's always spotless."

Cooper chuckled. "She'll never know I was there."

A few minutes after they disconnected, Cooper arrived at the loft apartment Kelly shared with his wife, Jen.

Kelly was waiting for him in the doorway. He'd changed out of his police uniform and into jeans and a T-shirt.

As Cooper regarded his brother, he saw himself as he had been four years ago. They shared the same dark hair and blue eyes, the same lanky, muscular build. Their mother liked to call them her almost-twins despite the difference in their ages.

"My favorite big brother," Kelly said, giving Cooper a hug. "Come in."

Cooper laughed at the old joke. "I'm your only brother."

"Details," Kelly scoffed. "Want a grape soda?"

"I'd love one."

"Have a seat," Kelly said, motioning to the living room. He walked into the gleaming kitchen.

Cooper plopped down on the brown leather sofa in front of the large window that made up one wall of the living room. The blinds were drawn against the afternoon sun.

Kelly returned with two glass bottles of grape soda. He handed one to Cooper, then sat on an armchair. "I was about to call you. I saw Kent at the station earlier today. He asked me how you were doing."

"Did he say why?"

"He told me there was another murder in that apartment house," Kelly replied. "Was it really the same apartment and everything?"

"Yeah." Cooper slumped into the couch cushions. "It happened exactly one year after Jill Kinner was killed there."

"It's hard to believe," Kelly said. "Do they have any suspects?"

"They picked up a guy," Cooper said. "Daryl Peters."

"You're wondering if you ID'd the wrong guy last time," Kelly said, studying him. "Aren't you?"

"I'm wondering if what I remember seeing last year might have been affected by getting shot in the head."

"You've been awfully sure all this time," Kelly reminded him. "The second murder isn't necessarily tied to the first."

"Really?" Cooper asked. "It was the same day, same apartment, and same type of murder."

"Okay, I see your point. Was Peters a suspect last time?"

"He was a person of interest," Cooper answered. "When they arrested Dane Wolff, they thought they already had the guilty man, so nobody checked into Peters very much."

"Wolff's playing it for all he's worth," Kelly said. "I heard his lawyers have already filed a motion to dismiss the charges for the first murder."

"Great. I'd be surprised if they don't at least postpone the trial until they find out more about the new case."

"Do you know anything about Peters?" Kelly asked. "Do you think he did it?"

"I don't know. That's why I went to see him today." Cooper told him about taking Jayla to talk to Peters at the detention facility.

When he got to the part about Peters being scratched by a strange woman wearing gardening gloves with claws, his brother scoffed. "You're joking."

"No joke. Have you ever come across anything like that?"

Kelly shook his head.

"Anyway, that's exactly what he said. I guess somebody in forensics would have taken a sample from those scratches to see if this other person left any traces of DNA on him."

"Which she wouldn't have if she was wearing gloves."

"True," Cooper said. "But Katie Myers would have if she was really the one who scratched him."

"Well, that should be fairly easy for them to check. And if Katie scratched him, she'd have his DNA under her fingernails too."

"Yeah, it should be easy," Cooper said.

"But that doesn't clear Wolff." Kelly cocked his head. "What are you thinking?"

"His wife hired me to look into the case again."

"No way," Kelly said. "And you agreed to do it?"

Cooper nodded. "Laurel has always claimed Wolff was at home with her the night of the first murder. She's right about Peters not being checked out very thoroughly at the time. Maybe he did kill both women."

"Isn't that something the department should investigate?" Kelly reminded him. "After all, it is our job."

"And it's my job to investigate whatever my client wants investigated," Cooper argued. "Don't tell me it's weird that she would hire me and not somebody else."

"Isn't it? You're the main witness against her husband."

"But I'm the one who was there the night of the murder he committed," Cooper added. "Well, allegedly committed. I'm the one who's been interviewed by the police and the district attorney about the case. I'm the one who's seen all the evidence there is against Wolff, and besides what I saw, there's precious little of it."

Kelly took a sip of his grape soda. "What about Jayla?"

"I shouldn't have taken her over there to talk to Peters," Cooper said with a sigh. "She's still struggling with what she heard that night last year."

"I take it she didn't recognize Peters's voice."

"No."

"Is Jayla okay?" Kelly asked. "About you, I mean."

Cooper frowned. "About me? I'm sure she never gives me a thought anymore."

"Come on," Kelly said. "Jayla was crazy about you, and you were crazy about her."

"*Was* being the operative word there," Cooper said. "She *was* crazy about me."

"And now?"

Cooper blew out a noisy breath. "She's still dealing with what happened last year. I'm sure I only remind her of that. I don't think it was a good idea to take her over to see Peters. I didn't realize until today how much hearing that first murder still bothers her. She told me she was having trouble sleeping. I assumed she'd be better a year after the fact. I never really considered that it could be otherwise."

"Maybe she's struggling because of this second murder," Kelly suggested. "I'd guess it rakes up everything about the first one again. Or she could be worried about something else that has nothing to do with either of the murders. You don't know."

Cooper took a drink of his soda. "Yeah."

"Unless, of course, you ask her." Kelly grinned.

"Don't say it. You've always thought I made a mistake when I let her go."

"It's true. One of the dumber things you've done, and that's saying something."

Cooper scowled at him. "Just because the four of us got along."

"We had some good times going out together, and Jen does feel a little outnumbered when she's stuck with you and me," Kelly said. "But what really matters is that I've never seen you so happy. Jen and I thought you were going to get married."

"I believed we would end up together too. But I don't know if I'm cut out for marriage. She's better off with someone she can depend on."

Kelly held up one hand. "I'm not getting into all that with you again. Your life, your choice."

Cooper drained the last of his grape drink and handed the bottle back to his brother. "Got another one?"

"That'll catch up with you." Kelly strolled into the kitchen, opened another grape soda, and brought it to Cooper. "You're not getting any younger."

"I'm not a cop anymore," Cooper said smugly. "Nobody cares if I'm in shape."

Kelly sat down again. "You don't look like you've missed too many days at the gym yet, but somehow I don't think you came by because you wanted to drink everything in my house."

"Not exactly," Cooper said, lifting the bottle and taking a drink. "I wanted to find out what you knew about the murder and ask you to call me if you learn anything else. You hear all the scuttlebutt."

"Most of it anyway." Kelly raised his eyebrows. "Does that mean you're going to give the department whatever you dig up? Fair's fair."

"Laurel Wolff is well aware that I believe her husband's guilty. There's no way she can possibly think I'd cover up anything I found against him, and if I discover evidence against someone else, I'm sure she'd want the police to know right away."

"Did you tell Stanley you're working for her?" Kelly asked.

"Not yet," Cooper said, "but I'll get around to it."

Kelly shrugged. "You're the boss of you."

"And don't you forget it." Cooper stood and raised his almost-full bottle. "Mind if I take this with me?"

"Help yourself." Kelly got up too. "You should come over for dinner sometime. I'll ask Jen to make her famous lasagna."

"That sounds good," Cooper said. "As long as she doesn't mind. I don't want to wear out my welcome."

"You know we're always glad to have you over," Kelly said. "For some reason, I enjoy your company, and Jen always worries about whether you're eating okay. Besides, we haven't seen you since Easter. That was more than a month ago."

Cooper hesitated. Had it really been that long?

"Come on," Kelly said. "You've been awfully hard to pin down the past few months."

"What are you talking about?" Cooper asked. "All you have to do is call."

"I don't mean we couldn't get ahold of you," Kelly told him. "But it's been hard to get you to come over. You used to stop by and hang out all the time. I've missed it."

Cooper felt a stab of guilt. He and Kelly had been best friends for almost their entire lives. Cooper had let his relationship with his brother slip lately. He'd let a lot of things slip.

He gave Kelly an affectionate punch on the arm. "Tell Jen I'll be over for dinner. Name the day, and let me know what to bring."

Kelly grinned and walked with him to the door. "Bring some grape soda."

Jayla was at the grocery store when her phone rang the next day.

Her heart skipped a beat when she saw Cooper's name on the display, and then she frowned and dismissed the call, putting her phone on silent. Was she mad at him or simply confused? Cooper had been so sweet and comforting after they'd gone to see Peters at the jail. He'd even admitted that he'd expected them to get married before—well, before everything. But he hadn't said he wanted to see her again. He'd only apologized. But it didn't really help anything. It didn't undo months of grief and pain.

Did she want to talk to him? Or did she want him to leave her alone? This murder case was his problem. Cooper had believed that he'd failed, but his feelings were on him. He wasn't her business anymore. He'd made sure of that.

But Cooper still cared about her. Jayla could hear it in his voice, see it in his eyes, and feel it in his touch. Despite his ridiculous idea that she was better off without him, she knew they cared for each other, but she didn't know what to do about it.

When Cooper had broken up with her, she had assumed that he would come to his senses within a few weeks. He hadn't.

Then Jayla had gotten angry and decided that Cooper deserved to be alone. She vowed to find someone else, but she hadn't even tried. It had become clear that she hadn't stopped loving him. There wasn't someone better for her. Still, Mary Ann was right. Jayla couldn't make Cooper come back, and she shouldn't waste her life expecting him to.

She checked her list to make sure she hadn't forgotten anything, then returned to the freezer section and grabbed a gallon of mint chocolate chip ice cream. She was going to need it.

After paying for her purchases, Jayla loaded her groceries into the car and turned up the air conditioner full force. Even with the window down a quarter inch, the interior of the car was really hot. She didn't like to think about what it would do to her ice cream.

It wasn't until she was ready to drive home that she listened to Cooper's message.

"I guess you're busy," he said. "I was hoping you might have lunch with me today, but it seems like I waited too long to ask."

It was already eleven thirty. Did he think she was sitting around, waiting for him to call?

"Anyway, I was hoping you'd see me," Cooper continued. "So we could talk some more. I realize that was hard on you yesterday, and I'd like to make it up to you. I want to know how you've been. Call me if you want."

Jayla pulled out of the parking space. She didn't have to call him back this second. She could drive home, put away the groceries, and then decide if she even wanted to talk to him. She reminded herself that her ice cream was already melting.

She phoned him on the way home anyway. "I saw you called," she said casually. "Sorry I couldn't answer. What's up?"

"You're just in time," Cooper said. "I was about to stick a couple pieces of leftover pizza into the microwave, but I'd rather take you to lunch."

Jayla didn't respond. She didn't know how to.

"I mean, if you'd like to go," he added. "I thought we could talk."

She still didn't answer. She should have figured out what to tell him before she'd called.

"I'm sorry about yesterday."

"Yesterday was fine. It wasn't that big of a deal." Jayla waited for him to argue with her. She knew she'd sounded like a spineless fool when she talked about listening to that 911 call.

"Will you have lunch with me?" Cooper asked. "I'm really hungry, and I'm not sure how long ago I bought this pizza."

She laughed. "I've got a bunch of groceries in the car. I have to get home before my ice cream melts."

"Mint chocolate chip?"

"Of course." Jayla wasn't surprised that he remembered her favorite flavor.

"What about a little later? Or do you want to call me when I can come pick you up?"

For a moment, she considered making an excuse. But then she realized that she wanted to see him again. She needed to know if there was still something special between them.

"All right," Jayla said. "I'll call you when I'm ready. And you decide where we're going, because I don't want to."

"Sushi?"

"What? You know we both hate raw fish."

He chuckled. "I'll surprise you, okay?"

"That sounds fun," she said. "Talk to you soon."

When Jayla got home, she carried two grocery bags into the kitchen. She immediately put the ice cream in the freezer, glad to see it hadn't melted too much.

Mary Ann entered the room and peeked into one of the bags.

"Do me a favor?" Jayla asked.

"Sure," Mary Ann said.

"There are a few more bags in the car. I'd really appreciate it if you'd bring them in and put everything away."

Mary Ann wrinkled her forehead. "Is something going on?"

"I have to go somewhere in a few minutes, and I need to get ready."

"How interesting." Mary Ann grinned. "Anybody I know?"

"Oh, stop. It's not like it's a date or anything. We're only going to talk."

Mary Ann wrinkled her nose in disgust. "You're going to talk about that murder case with Cooper."

Jayla rolled her eyes and marched toward her bedroom.

"Am I wrong?" Mary Ann called after her.

Jayla closed her bedroom door with more force than necessary.

Half an hour later, the doorbell rang, and Jayla hurried to answer it before her sister could get there. Fortunately, Mary Ann remained in her room.

"Thanks for joining me," Cooper said. "Are you ready to go?"

"Yes." She grabbed her purse and closed the door. "Where are we going?"

"It's a surprise." He ushered her to his car and opened the door for her.

Jayla slid into the passenger seat. "So you're not going to tell me?"

"You'll see when we get there," Cooper answered with a grin.

When they arrived at one of their favorite Tex-Mex restaurants, she smiled. Tex-Mex was one kind of food she and Cooper had always agreed on. For some reason, she hadn't had it much since they'd split up. "Good choice."

"I thought you'd like it." He got out and walked around the vehicle, then opened her door and escorted her into the restaurant.

It was crowded, but the hostess promptly seated them at a small table. She handed them two menus. "Your waitress will be right with you."

Sure enough, a waitress carrying a tray breezed over to their table. She introduced herself, then set a basket of tortilla chips, a small bowl of salsa, and two glasses of water on the table. "I'll be back in a minute for your order."

"Fajitas?" Cooper asked as he perused his menu.

Jayla grinned. "You know it."

"Extra queso, no sour cream, tomatoes, and lots of bell peppers?" he added.

Her grin widened.

"Steak, chicken, and shrimp?"

"Perfect," she said. "For two?"

"Of course," Cooper replied. "No way I'm letting you have all the good stuff."

"Good. I couldn't possibly eat a single serving all at once."

"I know," he said with a grin of his own. "And that leaves more for me."

Jayla shook her head as she studied him. He was as lean and sleek as ever. "It's not fair that you can eat so much and not gain an ounce."

"It's the Cole metabolism," he said smugly.

"And running most mornings," she said. "Don't forget."

Cooper laughed. "Okay, there's that too."

The waitress returned and took their order for fajitas. They both asked for glasses of iced tea as well.

After the waitress left, Cooper was silent as he snacked on chips and salsa.

Jayla wondered why he had invited her to lunch. Did he really have something to say to her? Or was it an excuse to see her again? No, that couldn't be possible. If Cooper missed her, then he would have contacted her before. There was no use getting her hopes up.

Finally, she got impatient. It was clear she'd have to start this conversation. "Well?"

"Well what?" he asked, raising his eyebrows.

"You said you wanted to talk," she reminded him. "I'm listening."

"I wanted to see how you're doing," Cooper said. "I didn't realize until yesterday how much you were struggling with what happened last year."

"I haven't been," Jayla said, absently stirring her water with a straw. "Not really. Not until the murder on Thursday night."

"I understand. I'm sorry."

She felt a flash of temper. "Stop saying you're sorry. You didn't kill her, did you?"

"Of course not, but—"

"Then stop apologizing."

They were interrupted when the waitress delivered their glasses of iced tea. "Your food will be out shortly."

Cooper didn't respond until the waitress hurried away to another table. "I let Jill die," he said, his voice hard. "I didn't protect her the way I should have. I didn't even keep the killer from getting away. And because of that, Katie's death is on my hands too."

"He shot you in the head," Jayla said. "What were you supposed to do? Drag yourself after him and tackle him around the knees?"

"I don't know. I only know I failed."

"It's not your fault," she assured him. "Stop blaming yourself."

"I wish it were that easy."

Jayla's heart went out to him. She wished she could say or do something to make him feel better.

They were silent for a few moments.

"I've missed you," he said quietly. "I really have."

"But not enough to call me in the last eight months."

"You know why. It's not because . . ." His voice trailed off.

*It's not because I don't love you.* Was that what was in his expression—or was it her own wishful thinking? "I know it's because you're sure I'm better off without such a loser."

Cooper shook his head. "That's not what I said."

"But it's what you meant." Jayla gave him a hard look. "Right?"

"There have been two murders, and I don't want that number to go up. But that's my problem, not yours. I shouldn't have asked you to relive this horrible ordeal. I guess I was hoping to catch a break on this case." He reached over and took her hand. "Forgive me?"

She felt herself warm at his touch, but she moved her hand away. "I think you're crazy, but I've always understood. We've both had a lot to work through. Then again, I thought it might have been easier for both of us if we'd tried to deal with it together."

"Yeah, maybe so."

Jayla wondered why he suddenly seemed to find the idea reasonable. But it didn't matter. His reaction didn't alter anything. It was too late for them. Their relationship was over.

She decided to change the subject. "Are you seeing anybody?" she asked, using a tortilla chip to scoop up some of the chunky salsa. "Besides Lizzie, I mean."

He chuckled. "Lizzie's great. She's already decided that she owns the house and everything in it. Including me."

Jayla crunched into her chip. "And nobody else has a claim on you?" She hoped she sounded completely nonchalant.

"No," Cooper said. "Not since I got out of the hospital."

That was eight months ago, when he had insisted it would be better for Jayla if she found someone else who hadn't quit his job and didn't know what he was going to do next. Someone who might be better at keeping people from dying.

"What about you?" he asked.

"Not really," she said. "I've gone on a couple of double dates with Mary Ann. She's been trying to fix me up, but she's even pickier than I am about who I go out with. I did one disastrous evening of speed dating. Never again."

Cooper laughed softly, but his smile didn't reach his eyes. "Sorry it hasn't worked out for you yet."

The waitress returned with an enormous iron skillet filled with steak, chicken, and shrimp along with onions, bell peppers, and tomatoes all grilled to perfection. She set the skillet in the middle of the table, warning them it was hot.

Jayla wanted to laugh because the fajitas were still sizzling. Instead, she told the waitress, "Thank you. They smell delicious."

The waitress set a plate of flour tortillas on the table along with a generous serving of chili con queso, rice, and beans. "Anything else I can get you?"

"I think we're good for now," Cooper said. He glanced at Jayla. "Anything we still need?"

Jayla shook her head.

"Enjoy your meals. I'll check on you in a little while," the waitress said, and then she left them alone.

They loaded their tortillas with the meats and vegetables along with rice and beans and queso. Jayla added a generous amount of salsa to hers, but she left the tomatoes for Cooper.

He shook his head. "I still don't get it. If you don't like tomatoes, why do you eat salsa? It's full of them."

"Hush and eat your food while it's still hot," she told him, pretending to be stern.

They made pleasant chitchat while they savored their food.

He finally leaned back and sighed. "That was great."

"Delicious," Jayla said, taking one last bite before she put down the remainder of the fajita she'd been eating. "But that's all I can eat."

"I'm glad you enjoyed it," Cooper said. "You appeared a little peaked yesterday."

"Is that why you asked me to have lunch with you?" she teased. "To fatten me up?"

"No, but I did want to make sure you were okay."

Jayla took a sip of her tea, annoyed to see the ice had mostly melted. "I'm fine."

"Then why aren't you looking at me?"

"I'm fine. Really." She forced herself to meet his eyes. "I don't want you to feel like you have to babysit me because of what's happening."

He crossed his arms over his chest. "What do you mean?"

"You wouldn't be around otherwise," Jayla said, her tone harsher than she intended. "Don't lie."

"I never said I didn't care about you. I—"

She cut him off. "You abandoned me." She had to draw a slow, deep breath to get ahold of herself.

"I told you why it was best if we didn't stay together," Cooper said.

"You did. I'm sorry. I'm just terrified, and I wish—" Jayla bit her lip, not allowing herself to say the words out loud. She would have liked for him to have been around last night. Maybe then she wouldn't have had nightmares about gloves with claws.

"Is it about this new murder?" he asked. "Or is something else going on?"

She toyed with her napkin and didn't answer.

"Talk to me," Cooper said, his voice low and urgent. "Please let me help you. I know I left you hanging, but it was because I couldn't deal with everything. Let me help you now, okay?"

Maybe it wasn't love. Maybe it was simply guilt and regret. His tendency to take care of everybody who required it. She couldn't deny that she needed that from him.

"It's not anything in particular," Jayla said. "It's everything. I thought I was moving on from last year and things were going well. I guess the only way for me to get past it is to take some control over the situation."

He raised one dark eyebrow. "And?"

She squared her shoulders. "Are you going to see Peters again?"

"I'm planning to," Cooper answered. "I haven't asked him very much about the Kinner murder yet, and it's possible he had something to do with it."

"When are you going?" she asked, forcing her voice to stay calm and even. "After lunch?"

"I can. Why?"

Jayla took a deep breath. "I want to go with you."

Daryl Peters was clearly surprised to see Cooper and Jayla again. He snatched up the receiver. "Something's happened. Did you find the real killer?"

"We're still investigating," Cooper said into the receiver. "We wanted to ask you a few more questions. Mostly about the murder last year."

Jayla leaned closer to the receiver Cooper held so she could hear what Peters said.

Peters sighed. "I don't know anything about it."

"There might be a detail that could help," Cooper said. "Why don't you start at the beginning?"

Peters ran one hand through his thinning hair. "My wife, Marie, passed away a couple of days before Jill Kinner was murdered."

"I'm sorry," Cooper told him. "That must have been rough."

"I was in such a daze, and I couldn't tell you where I was half the time," Peters said. "Mostly I was at home by myself. We didn't have any kids."

"I understand you live close to Mrs. Calvin's apartment house," Cooper said. "Is that right?"

Peters nodded. "I live in a duplex a couple of blocks over. I inherited the building from my parents. I wouldn't be able to afford to live in that neighborhood otherwise."

"Do you know your neighbor on the other side?" Cooper asked.

"Yes, Ray Jensen. He's a real nice man." Peters switched the receiver from one ear to the other. "Anyway, that night was like most of them were back then. I couldn't sleep, so I walked."

"Walked where?" Jayla asked.

"Around the house."

"You didn't walk outside?" Cooper asked.

"No," Peters said. "Even at night, it's too hot most of the time. If I can't sleep, I walk around the house. Sometimes I drink coffee. It's supposed to keep you awake, but it doesn't work that way for me."

"Why do you drink it then?" Cooper asked.

"It makes me feel better," Peters answered. "It reminds me of Marie. She used to brew coffee for us, and we'd sit up late and talk."

"Sure," Cooper said. "Is that something you still do?"

"Not always, but lately I've been missing Marie so much. Around the anniversary of her death, I kept thinking about her. I imagined I'd glance up, and she'd be sitting there doing her cross-stitch and sipping coffee." Peters gazed at them, his pale eyes brimming with tears. "Now that she's gone, nobody else in the world cares what happens to me. I'll never stop missing her."

Jayla put her hand on the glass between them. He might be a murderer, but she wasn't sure she believed it. He looked so lost and frightened that she wished she could put her arms around him and comfort him. "I'll pray for you," she said softly.

Peters swiped his eyes with his denim sleeve and smiled apologetically. "Thank you. I need that more than ever."

"Can anyone verify that you were home the night of the murder last year?" Cooper asked. "Maybe your neighbor?"

"I don't think so," Peters said.

"Do you remember anything else about that night?" Cooper asked. "Do you recall what else you did besides walk around the house?"

Peters hesitated as he considered the question. "No, I can't think of anything."

"I'm still working on this case," Cooper told him. "The police are too. So the more you can tell us, the better off you'll be. Even if you're guilty, if you tell us the truth, we can get you the help you need."

"What are you saying?" Peters asked, recoiling. "That I'm crazy?"

"Of course not," Cooper assured him. "We simply want to know who murdered those women and why."

"I hope you find out. I really do." Peters clutched the receiver. "Thanks for what you're doing."

"We'll be back to see you if we come up with any more questions," Cooper said.

Peters nodded.

"I should stop at the station and talk to Stanley," Cooper said as he escorted Jayla through the detention facility. "Do you want me to drop you off at home first?"

"No, that's okay," she said. "I'll tag along."

As they walked out to Cooper's car, Jayla considered Peters. He seemed so bewildered and harmless that it was hard to picture him actually hurting anyone. It was impossible to imagine him being the source of that horrible hissing, growling voice she had heard as Jill Kinner was being murdered.

"I don't think it was Peters," she announced.

Cooper raised his eyebrows. "What?"

"I don't think it was Peters on the 911 call last year."

"Are you sure?" he asked, opening the passenger door for her.

"Maybe not completely," she said as she slid into the seat. "But I honestly don't think so."

Cooper didn't respond. He walked around the vehicle and got behind the wheel.

Jayla regarded him. "Do you think he is?"

"I'm not sure. He mentioned that after his wife died, he walked around his house in the middle of the night and didn't know where he was half the time. Could he have possibly zoned out and walked over to Mrs. Calvin's and killed Jill Kinner? It would have been shortly after his wife's death."

"And then you think he did the same thing on the anniversary of her death?" Jayla shook her head. "That's a pretty wild theory."

"Wilder things have happened," he said. "What about his voice?"

"I don't know," she admitted. "Not the way he usually talks anyway. But I guess anybody could hiss and growl."

"Yeah, especially if he was having some kind of psychotic break."

Jayla didn't like to think a kindly man like Peters would kill two women, but maybe he had.

And maybe he wasn't even aware of it.

"I hate to ask you this," Cooper said as he drove away from the detention facility. "But is there anything you remember from the Kinner murder that you haven't told the police? Anything at all?"

Jayla gripped the padded armrest and squeezed her eyes shut. "When Katie Myers was killed, I wondered if it would dredge up memories from Jill Kinner's murder. But I don't recall anything else."

"Have you done anything to jog your memory?" he asked. "Like reading the transcript of the 911 call?"

"I've read the transcript before," she said. "I can handle the words, even as horrible as they were, but I don't want to remember the sounds or how it felt. I worked too hard to forget it after Jill Kinner was murdered. I can't do it."

"There were a few places marked 'unintelligible' on that transcript," Cooper said, glancing over at her. "Do you remember anything that was missing?"

"No. Most of it is blank, and when I try to make myself remember, it doesn't work. I guess my subconscious doesn't want to go there. I can't help it."

"It's all right," he said. "I understand."

Jayla bit her lip, feeling the same queasiness she always got when she thought of that particular night and the man on the phone. But now another woman had been killed. The murderer needed to be stopped before it happened again.

She took a deep breath. "If I listened to the tape again, perhaps I'd be able to figure out some of those unintelligible places in the recording."

"I don't know if that's a good idea." Cooper slowed to a stop at a red light and peered at her. "Stanley could probably arrange for us to listen to it, but is that something you want to put yourself through? This has been hard enough for you already. What if it makes things worse?"

"You'd better take me up on it before I change my mind," Jayla said with a weak laugh. She gestured to the nearest street sign. "We're almost at the station."

"You should think about it pretty hard," he advised. "What if I listen to it instead? Maybe I'll be able to figure out something else about the transcript."

"That wouldn't be much help," she said. "You didn't hear the guy on the 911 call last year."

"But maybe I could decipher some of the unintelligible parts."

Jayla smirked. "Yeah, because the people who couldn't are only experts who work with this kind of thing all the time. Why wouldn't you be better at it?"

Cooper rolled his eyes.

The light turned green. He stepped on the gas and headed toward the station.

"I'm not looking forward to this," she confessed, her tone softer, "but it's something that needs to be done. If it ends up being too much, I'll walk out. I might even decide you're on your own on this case if I can't cope with it. But we won't be able to tell until I try. And I have to try."

He drove to the station and pulled into the parking lot, not saying anything else.

"You understand, don't you?" she asked.

Cooper switched off the engine. "Yeah, because neither of us wants this to happen again the next time somebody rents apartment four."

When they entered the station, Sheila Raymond, the receptionist, was not at her desk. They walked to the back of the building and found Stanley having an animated conversation with another officer.

Stanley laughed, slapped the other cop on the back, and faced Cooper and Jayla. "What are you two up to?"

"We went to talk to Peters about last year," Cooper said.

"What did he say?" Stanley asked.

"Not a lot," Cooper replied. "He still claims he didn't have anything to do with killing anybody, but it's an old cliché, isn't it? The mild-mannered guy who wouldn't swat a fly ends up being a mass murderer. Is he getting any kind of psych evaluation?"

"Definitely," Stanley said. "Why?"

"He admitted he was in a daze after losing his wife," Cooper said. "He told us that he was probably walking around his house the night of the murder. He was home alone, so he has no alibi."

Stanley nodded. "We've been over that. Then and now. We're still checking him out, especially in light of what happened last week."

"So what's his motive?" Cooper asked. "Why do you think he would murder Kinner and Myers?"

"Who can say?" Stanley asked. "Maybe he'd been watching the young women in the apartments he maintained for a long time. He murdered one, then realized he couldn't stop. We picked him up because of the physical evidence. We'll figure out why."

"Do you think he's insane?" Jayla asked.

"I'm leaving that to the psychiatrists," Stanley said. "So what brings you two here?"

"We wanted to give you the update on Peters," Cooper said.

"And I want to listen to the 911 recording from last year," Jayla said. "Maybe I can match the voices or figure out something that was missed."

Stanley studied her for a moment. "Are you sure? I thought you refused to listen to the tape last year."

"Things have changed," Jayla said. "I think I can handle it this time. I want to at least try."

"Do you have time today?" Stanley asked. "It may take a few minutes to track it down."

"What do you think?" Cooper asked Jayla.

"I've got time," she replied.

"Great," Stanley said. "Tell Sheila to put you in one of the interview rooms. I'll get the tape and join you."

"Thanks." Cooper took Jayla's arm. "We'll be waiting."

They walked over to Sheila's desk and waited for her to finish the phone call she was taking.

The receptionist hung up, then turned to them with her usual smile. "Hi there," she said to Cooper. "When are you going to marry me?"

Sheila was somewhere between fifty and sixty, and she regularly used the line on almost all the men who worked at the station.

Cooper winked at her. "When your husband says I can."

"You go ask Max," Sheila said, rolling her dark eyes. "I'm sure he'll tell you to haul me off anytime."

Jayla laughed. "That's not true. Max wouldn't have a clue what to do without you. How's he doing?"

Sheila and Max had been married for more than thirty years, and Jayla knew how important he was to her. He had been diagnosed with lung cancer, and he'd been in treatment for months. He'd gone into remission, and it had appeared that he was going to defeat the disease. Unfortunately, it had recently returned. Max had never smoked, but his parents had, and now he was paying the price.

"He has his good days and bad days. There's always some new medication to try." Sheila sighed. "New and expensive. I couldn't tell you how many hours I've spent on the phone with the insurance company. Evidently our policy covers everything except what we need most."

Jayla winced. "That's awful."

"The head of the finance department at our doctor's office is trying to get the hospital to write off some of their charges," Sheila continued. "She said if they don't, she's going to tell them she won't schedule his next surgery with them."

"I'm so sorry," Jayla said. "I was hoping they'd gotten it all last time."

Sheila shook her head. "I'm praying they'll get it this time."

"I'm sorry. I had no idea you guys were dealing with all of that." Cooper leaned on the desk. "How's Max taking it?"

"He's hanging in there," Sheila answered. "He says attitude is everything. He drinks orange juice and watches a lot of movies. Who knows? Maybe he'll surprise the doctors and everybody else."

"I'm pulling for him," Cooper said. "He's tough. He can beat it."

"Neither of us will go down without a fight. I'll do whatever it takes to get him through this." Sheila smiled. "Well, enough about that. What brings you my way?"

"Stanley said you'd let us use an interview room for a few minutes," Cooper told her. "Do you have one free?"

"Come this way." Sheila rounded the desk and led them down the corridor. She rested her hand on Jayla's shoulder. "I thought you were working today."

"No, I have the day off. We were in the area and needed to go over some evidence in a case."

Sheila glanced from Cooper to Jayla, a knowing look on her face. "Are you taking up private investigations?"

Jayla kept from blushing—barely—and managed an offhand shrug instead. "I'm only helping out temporarily. I was involved in a related case, so I thought I might be able to do some good on this one."

"Not that murder case in the apartment house, is it?" Sheila asked, sobering.

Jayla nodded.

"Stanley told me about it, and it gives me the creeps," Sheila said with a shudder. "I don't know if it's possible that a second murder in the same apartment and on the anniversary of the first one is a coincidence."

"That's how I feel too," Cooper said.

Sheila opened the door to a small room with a table and a few chairs in it.

"Thanks for letting us use the room," Cooper said.

"No problem. Make yourselves at home." Sheila headed back down the hall.

Cooper stepped aside so Jayla could enter the room first. He closed the door behind them.

She sank into a chair. It was old and hard and ugly. Like her thoughts.

"Are you sure you're okay with this?" Cooper asked, sitting down beside her.

"I'm sure."

"How about something to drink? A cup of coffee? A soda?"

"Yeah, coffee would be good," Jayla answered. "Thanks."

He left and came back a couple of minutes later with two full cups and a few small containers of cream and sugar.

Cooper put cream into his cup, and Jayla added sugar to hers. They drank in silence for a short time, and she closed her eyes, letting the liquid warmth soak into her body and smooth out the tangles in her nerves.

"I'm sorry that you have to keep going over the murder," he said eventually. "I can't imagine how difficult it's been."

"No. It's fine. Keeping all this buried might be why it never goes away."

"That's possible."

Jayla wondered if Cooper had been right to break up with her after all. It was possible that neither one of them was fit to be in a relationship at this point. Not until they had dealt with both murders and let it all go. Although he didn't say anything else, she could tell he was thinking the same thing.

They had both soldiered on. The weight of the baggage hadn't crippled either one of them, but it had certainly slowed them down. It might be time to put that baggage down, open it up, and see if there was anything in there they actually needed to keep.

"You're not making me do something I don't want to do," she assured him. "I'm tired of letting this incident hold on to me."

"If you need me, I'll be here," he said, his voice as smooth and warm as the coffee.

Jayla tried to focus on that voice from the 911 call and not the one she was about to hear. Maybe over time she had made that other voice more horrible than it actually had been. Maybe she had somehow mixed it up with some of the scary movies she'd seen when she was a kid. Maybe—

The door flew open, and she started, sloshing a few drops of hot coffee on her hand.

"I'm sorry," Stanley said. "I didn't mean to scare you."

"Not a problem," Jayla said.

Cooper gave her the napkin he had around his cup, and she blotted the coffee from her hand.

Stanley pulled up a chair that was against the wall. "I've got some bad news."

"What?" Cooper asked.

"The 911 recording from the Kinner case is gone."

Cooper stared at Stanley, unable to believe what he had heard. "What do you mean the tape is gone?"

"It's missing," Stanley said, with more than a little irritation. "As in, not there anymore. Not anywhere."

"I thought it had been locked up since last year," Cooper said. "What happened?"

"I wish I could tell you," Stanley said. "It was there a couple of months ago. One of Wolff's defense attorneys wanted to listen to it. I got it for him and put it back myself. I've gone through the records. It hasn't been checked out. It should be where I left it, but it's not there. I have no idea where it went."

Cooper glanced at Jayla. She was white to the gills. He couldn't say for sure whether it was from fear about what was going on or merely relief that she didn't have to listen to the recording of that 911 call.

"What about the transcript?" Jayla asked.

"It's gone too," Stanley said. "But I can request another copy. Whoever typed it will have it in the computer."

"We hope," Cooper said. "If nothing else, the DA's office and the defendant's attorneys will have copies."

"I hadn't thought of that," Stanley said. "I'll make some calls." He faced Jayla. "Sorry. It seems like you came here for nothing."

Jayla drained her coffee cup, then gave him a smile. "It's okay. To be honest, I'm glad I didn't have to listen to that tape after all. I might give it another try when it turns up again. Hopefully I'll be a little more prepared by then."

"It would have been nice to either have made the connection with Peters to that tape or ruled it out," Stanley said thoughtfully. "I don't suppose there's anything you've remembered about the 911 call on your own."

Jayla shook her head. "I spent most of the past year trying to make myself forget, but now I'm trying to remember. I'm sorry, but I haven't thought of anything new so far."

"It's not a problem," Stanley told her. "We'd better get used to the idea that you're never going to remember more than you've already told us. Maybe that's best anyway."

Cooper frowned. That didn't sound like Stanley at all. He was usually the type to tell a witness to keep thinking until he or she came up with something. But he was probably trying to keep from worrying Jayla. Cooper would have intervened if the officer had tried to push her around. Even for a good cause.

Cooper stood and nodded at Jayla. "Come on. I'll take you home."

"Sounds good," she said as she got up.

"Thanks for everything," Cooper said to Stanley. "Catch you later."

"Sure," Stanley said, then addressed Jayla. "Be careful. If you remember something, I want you to let me know immediately."

"I will," she said.

Cooper and Jayla left the room, then walked down the corridor, waved goodbye to Sheila, and headed to his car.

"You still have that pistol?" he asked as he opened the door for her. She stared at him. "Why?"

"I'm sure it's nothing, but I'd like to make sure you're safe."

She nodded as she slid into the car. "I go to the range every week. If I need to use it, I can."

"I hope you never need to, but I'm glad you have it just in case."

Cooper shut her door, then walked around and got behind the wheel. It was a short drive back to her place, and they managed to keep up an inconsequential conversation. The idea of leaving Jayla and her sister in the house alone was about to drive him crazy, but he kept those thoughts to himself. He had given up the right to say anything at all. At least she wouldn't be totally unprotected.

He'd seen Jayla at the range before. She was coolheaded and accurate. That and her continued practice made it likely that she would keep calm in any emergency where she needed to defend herself and Mary Ann.

"I talked to Kelly yesterday," he said since it was the only thing he could think of at the moment.

"Did you?" Jayla asked.

Evidently she wasn't going to even try to make this any easier for him. "Yeah, he and Jen are doing fine."

"Good," she said blandly. "Anything new with them? Any kids on the way?"

"According to Kelly, that's not in the plan. Not for a long while."

"That's what Jen told me last year. I didn't know if their plans had changed." Jayla shrugged. "But as they say, man plans and God laughs."

Cooper snickered. "I'd be laughing too. Especially at the look on Kelly's face when Jen broke the news to him."

Jayla didn't crack a smile. "I'll bet he'll be a great dad."

"Oh, no doubt. After he finished freaking out." He fell silent again. He was pretty sure she was thinking of their plans more than Kelly and Jen's. They'd come unraveled pretty fast last year.

"I asked him to keep me posted on anything he hears about the cases we're investigating," Cooper remarked. "Maybe he'll have something for us before long."

"Us?" she asked.

He raised an eyebrow at her. "Didn't you say you wanted to be kept in the loop?"

"I did, but I didn't know if you were sure about it."

"I'm sure I want you involved," Cooper said. "Because of what happened last year, we both have a unique perspective on this new case. Whether or not it'll come in handy, I can't say yet, but we need to use every advantage we have when we have it."

"I meant it when I said I want to help," Jayla insisted. "What can I do besides try to remember more details about the 911 call?"

"That's your main focus," he said. "And come up with brilliant theories about the case."

She smiled but didn't reply.

"Lizzie finally came out from under the bed," Cooper said, changing the subject. "I woke up this morning with her standing on my chest and staring down at me. At least she's acknowledged me as the source of food."

"Poor little thing," Jayla said. "It might take time for her to completely recover from what happened."

"You never did go with me to get her some toys," he reminded her.

"I guess we got distracted by other things," she said.

Cooper couldn't tell if that was uncertainty or regret in her expression. Jayla had plenty of reason for either, with a little wariness and mistrust thrown in for good measure. He'd definitely blown it with her. But no matter how much he told himself it was better for her to find someone else, he was glad she hadn't. He'd missed her. It was amazing how much they still connected even after nearly a year's estrangement. Although her family understandably disliked him these days, he couldn't help wondering what they would think if he asked her out again.

Still, he couldn't go there with her. Not until he figured out who had killed Katie Myers and how that was connected to the murder of Jill Kinner. And even then, it could only be if Jayla wanted to try again. Maybe once this was all over, she'd be glad she was free of him.

"Do you want to go shopping now?" Cooper asked, allowing himself the tiniest hint of a smile.

Jayla glanced at her watch.

"Come on," he urged. "The pet store is on the way to your house. It wouldn't take long to pick out something for Lizzie. What do you say?"

"Okay," she said finally. "That would be fun. But we are staying far away from the cats and dogs that are up for adoption, okay? I always end up wanting to take at least one home with me."

"I remember." Cooper chuckled. "But you can come visit Lizzie sometime if you want."

Jayla shook her head. "You probably won't have her for long. I don't want to get attached."

He let out a long, slow breath. "She hasn't been staying with me for that long, but I know I'm going to miss her."

"That's why I could never foster kittens," she said. "I'd always want to keep them. All of them."

Cooper smiled. She was still as kindhearted as ever.

When they arrived at the pet store, they ended up looking at the pets up for adoption anyway. It was Jayla's idea. Then they checked out all the fish and birds and hamsters that were for sale. Finally, they made it to the cat supplies at the rear of the store. Cooper purchased a few catnip mice with long tails, a couple of rubber balls, and a brightly colored stuffed trout.

"They're all small enough for Lizzie to carry around with her," he said once they were heading toward Jayla's place again.

Jayla took the colorful trout out of the bag and studied it. "She should love this. She might not appreciate the crazy colors, but she'll have a good time playing with it."

"We could have gotten her one of the little stuffed vets to kick around," he said with a chuckle.

"I think the trout is perfect," she said. "You know what we had for our cat when I was growing up?"

At that moment, Cooper's phone rang.

He checked the screen. "Excuse me for a second. It's Kelly." He answered. "What's up?"

"I thought you'd like to hear what Stanley found out," Kelly said. "You got time?"

"Sure. I'm in the car with Jayla. Can I put you on speaker?"

"If she's helping you on this, she might as well hear it too."

"Go ahead," Cooper said when he switched to speakerphone.

"Can you hear me, Jayla?" Kelly asked.

"Loud and clear," she said. "How are you?"

"Doing great. Jen and I were wondering how you've been. You should come hang out sometime."

"Yeah, sounds good," Jayla said, but she didn't sound too certain about the idea.

"Anyway, here's what I got from Stanley," Kelly said. "The preliminary reports on the Myers case say that the DNA evidence under the victim's nails matches Daryl Peters. Apparently, there was some attempt to wash the victim's hands before the assailant left the scene, but he didn't do a very thorough job because there was still DNA."

Cooper frowned and glanced at Jayla. She appeared disappointed. He knew she'd pitied the guy after they'd gone to see him. She must have hoped that he hadn't had anything to do with the killings.

"So those scratches on his neck were definitely from the victim?" Cooper asked his brother.

"That's a bit trickier," Kelly admitted. "Peters definitely was scratched around the time of the Myers murder. Those scratches were examined when he was arrested, but by then they were clean. He'd treated them with peroxide shortly after he was scratched, then put an antibiotic cream on them a few times. So, if there had been any DNA material from the victim on him, it would have been completely washed away."

"What about his story about somebody coming up and scratching him?" Jayla asked.

"That's a pretty crazy story," Kelly said. "I guess it's possible, but with his DNA being on the victim, I doubt that story is going to hold any weight with the DA or a jury. Do you buy it, Cooper?"

"I'm not buying anything yet," Cooper told him. "There's too much crazy going on here already."

Kelly chuckled. "Tell me about it. Well, that's all I've got for the moment. Do you two have anything new to add?"

"We've been buying cat toys," Jayla crowed, obviously enjoying letting Kelly know his brother hadn't exactly been tending to business.

"Cat toys," Kelly repeated. "Great job, Cooper. Way to dig up the truth there."

"We're on it," Cooper insisted. "We just—" He stopped when the phone beeped to tell him he had another call. It was Laurel Wolff. "I have to go," he told his brother. "Anything else I need to know?"

"No, that's pretty much it," Kelly said. "Talk to you later."

Cooper answered the other call and greeted Laurel. "What can I do for you?"

"I was hoping you could meet me at your office," Laurel said. "I've been to see my husband at the detention facility, and he asked me to get an update from you. There's also something important I need to speak to you about. Are you available?"

He was relieved that they were close to the office. "I could meet you in about half an hour, if that would work for you."

"I was hoping you'd be at your office," Laurel said, clearly displeased. "I have an appointment later on, so I have a small window of time to talk to you."

Jayla tapped his arm to get his attention and mouthed, "Tell her yes."

"I'm actually almost at my office right now," he said. "I'll meet you there."

"Thank you," Laurel said. "I should be there in less than ten minutes." She ended the call.

"I'm supposed to be helping you," Jayla reminded him. "I want to hear what she has to say too."

"I didn't know if you wanted to get home instead."

"I don't have to work tonight, remember?"

"I remember." Cooper paused. "Have you ever met Laurel?"

"No, but I've seen her on the news," she said. "How are you going to introduce me?"

"I'll tell her that you're working with me," he replied.

"Do you think she'll have a problem with that?" Jayla asked.

"No, it'll be fine," Cooper assured her.

But he couldn't ignore a feeling of dread settling in the pit of his stomach. He hoped he wasn't making a big mistake.

A few minutes after Jayla and Cooper arrived at his office, Laurel walked through the door.

Jayla couldn't help admiring the woman. Laurel wore a white blouse, a sleek black skirt, black pumps, and designer sunglasses. She was the epitome of refinement, composure, and complete certainty of her own worth and abilities. She didn't have to say a word about any of that, of course. It emanated from her like the subtle fragrance of lilies.

"Right on time," Cooper said, extending his hand. "Come in."

Laurel took his hand, her large diamond ring catching the sliver of sunlight that somehow slipped through the closed window blinds. "Thank you for seeing me on such short notice. I'll pay you for the inconvenience. You can put it on my bill."

"It's no problem," he said. "We were practically here already anyway."

Laurel gave Jayla a small, frosty smile. "And this is?"

"Jayla Randall," Cooper said. "She's helping me with your case."

Her lips, which perfectly matched her nail polish, turned up a little more. "Ah, the girlfriend. It's a pleasure to meet you at last."

"Cooper and I aren't dating anymore," Jayla clarified, "but I'm surprised you know about me at all."

Still smiling, Laurel looked expectantly at Cooper.

He immediately brought her a chair.

"Evidently my information isn't completely accurate," Laurel said. "But I know that you were the 911 operator who took the call when

93

that murder occurred last year, the one my husband was blamed for. I had heard that you have a different job now. Police dispatch?"

"That's right," Jayla said, feeling slightly unnerved by her cool certainty. "I hope you don't mind my asking, but how did you know?"

"There is more than one private investigator in Dallas," Laurel said, smoothing her skirt. "Once my husband was arrested last year, I employed several of them to find out what they could about all the people involved in the case. I want my husband to have every advantage in fighting this charge, and as they say, knowledge is power."

"Would you like something to drink?" Cooper asked. "I have coffee and bottled water."

"No thank you," Laurel answered. "I'm about to have cocktails with some business associates."

Cooper sat in the chair behind the desk. "So what can I do for you?"

"I understand Daryl Peters has been arrested for the murder of Katie Myers," Laurel began.

"He has," he said.

"Have you checked into his background and his alibi?" Laurel asked. "Do you know where he was during the Kinner murder?"

"I'm not entirely convinced that he's guilty," Cooper said, "but I'm still seeking information about him."

"Have the police questioned him about last year?" Laurel continued. "If he's guilty of this murder, it seems likely that he's guilty of the other one, doesn't it? I told you Dane couldn't have done it in the first place. He was at home with me."

"We have a long way to go on the case yet," he told her. "There are a lot of inconsistencies regarding the murders. You need to give me more time to investigate both of them."

"Inconsistencies?" Laurel asked, tilting her head. The diamond solitaire in her ear glinted in the ray of sunlight that fell over her shoulder. "Are you referring to the 911 tape disappearing from evidence at the police station?"

"You found out about that?" Cooper asked, obviously surprised.

Laurel nodded. "That's the main reason I wanted to talk to you. I tried to get permission to listen to it myself because I was hoping to prove that it wasn't Dane in the recording. But the police told me it was unavailable. I finally got them to admit they didn't know where it was, but they said it would be found."

"I'm sure they'll see to it," he said.

Laurel turned to Jayla, as if she expected her to explain the breach in security. "How can something like that happen? I thought the tape was locked up. After all, it is evidence."

"It should have been secure," Cooper said. "The officer in charge of the case is checking into it."

"Yes, Officer Stanley," Laurel said.

Jayla hid her surprise. Laurel certainly knew a great deal about her husband's case and everything to do with it.

"I want to know what happened to the recording," Laurel said, her dark eyes blazing. "I'm sure that wasn't my husband's voice on it. Someone else must have realized it too. What other reason could anyone have for stealing it?"

"Hopefully it will be found soon," Jayla said.

"I want you to make that part of your investigation," Laurel told Cooper. "I want the tape recovered before Dane goes to trial."

"Don't worry," he said. "I plan to track it down."

"Good. I expect you to locate it as quickly as possible," Laurel said. "Our attorneys are trying to get the trial postponed. How can they possibly try our case when this new one has so much bearing on it?"

"That's a matter for your legal team," Cooper said. "My job is to get as much information as I can."

"How do you fit into all this?" Laurel asked Jayla. "Are you also a licensed private investigator?"

Jayla hated the warmth that crept up her neck. She was sure Laurel would look down on her for it. Clearly she did anyway. "No, I'm only helping. Since Cooper and I both have connections to the Kinner case, we thought we could accomplish more together."

"Yes," Laurel said, studying her as if she hadn't actually noticed her before. "I understand Mr. Cole had some health issues after the incident."

"He's perfectly fine now," Jayla assured her. "He's helping me try to remember things too."

"What do you mean?" Laurel asked, frowning slightly.

Jayla hesitated as she searched for the words to explain.

"You've read the transcript," Cooper said to his client. "It's not a very easy thing to go through as it is. Jayla listened to that as it was happening. It's understandable that she would want to block as much as possible out of her mind."

"Of course," Laurel said, a note of sympathy in her voice. "Why are you trying to remember?"

"I don't want the wrong man to be convicted," Jayla responded. "Now that there's been a second murder, I feel compelled to try to help. There's a connection that I haven't made yet. I hope I can make that connection if I go through the evidence in both murders."

"Then I hope you succeed," Laurel said, "because whatever you discover will prove my husband is innocent and Daryl Peters is the real killer." She stood up and settled her purse on her shoulder, then faced Cooper. "I'll be waiting to hear from you. I want to know everything you uncover."

Cooper got to his feet. "I'll do that." He opened the door for her. With a nod to Jayla, Laurel left.

Cooper shut the door after her, locking it this time. Instead of returning to his desk, he sat down next to Jayla. "And that's Mrs. Laurel Wolff."

"She certainly makes an impression," Jayla told him.

"Yeah, Wolff is lucky she's on his side," he said. "If she was holding a grudge over his girlfriend, she could make things awfully hot for him."

"I guess she could. But don't you think it's strange that she's so forgiving about Jill Kinner?"

"What do you mean?"

"Jill wasn't just her husband's fling. He rented an apartment for her. If my husband did that to me, I wouldn't be very nice about it, and she doesn't seem all that warm and fuzzy to me anyway."

"Sometimes it's hard to tell about people," Cooper reasoned. "She's all ice sometimes."

Jayla raised an eyebrow at him.

"Okay, maybe most of the time," he said. "But she told me that she and her husband were making up after a long time of not getting along. He had ended things with Jill, and they were finally working out their marriage. Laurel claimed she had already forgiven him before Jill was killed. If that's the case, it makes sense that she would stand by him now, don't you think?"

Jayla exhaled. "It makes perfect sense, but I wish I knew who took that recording. Laurel thinks it would prove her husband was innocent. I don't know how that could be, since the voice I heard was very strange. Not a normal voice. I can't imagine anyone talking that way all the time. But if that recording is gone for good, I guess we'll never know."

"If it was Peters both times, then how could he have arranged for that recording to be stolen?" Cooper asked. "The Wolffs have all kinds of resources. They could have bribed someone to get rid of the recording.

But Peters isn't wealthy. When we talked to him, he mentioned that the only way he can afford to live in that neighborhood is because he inherited the duplex from his parents."

"I'm worried about him not having an alibi," Jayla admitted. "And he didn't remember very much about the night of the first murder. Don't you think that's strange?"

"It's not like he blacked out or anything," Cooper answered. "He says he was at home the whole time."

"But he can't prove it."

"Then maybe we can. I'd like to talk to Mrs. Calvin about him tomorrow morning. Perhaps we can pay Ray Jensen a visit too. It might be useful to talk to Peters's neighbor. Do you still want to help?"

Did she want to keep doing this? Jayla feared she was getting attached to Cooper again. He wanted her assistance with the case. He didn't want to get back together with her. She didn't want to let herself imagine that there could be something more between them. The last thing she needed was more heartbreak. And yet . . .

She nodded, hoping she wouldn't regret it.

The next morning Jayla woke up early after another fitful night's sleep.

As she waited for Cooper to arrive, she ate a bowl of cereal and sipped coffee at the table.

Mary Ann walked in and poured herself a cup of coffee. Then she leaned against the counter and studied her sister. "Where are you going?"

"Cooper and I are going to talk to the landlady where the murders happened," Jayla replied.

"I'm worried about you," Mary Ann said. "I don't want to see you get hurt again."

"I won't," Jayla said. "But I appreciate your concern."

The doorbell rang.

"I need to go." Jayla got up and put her empty bowl and cup in the sink. "I'll see you later."

"Be careful," Mary Ann said.

"I will." Jayla grabbed her purse in the living room and opened the front door. "Good morning."

Cooper smiled. "Thanks for coming with me."

"No problem," she said.

He ushered her to the car and opened the door for her. As they drove to the hotel where Mrs. Calvin was staying, they made small talk.

Jayla laughed as Cooper told her about Lizzie's antics with her new toys.

When they arrived at the hotel, Cooper drove into the lot and parked.

"This is amazing," Jayla said as they walked to the front entrance. The large hotel was sleek and modern. She guessed there were twenty stories.

He nodded. "Mrs. Calvin's buyers wanted to start remodeling right away. If you ask me, I think they wanted to get the work done while this whole investigation was happening, so they could rent those apartments out as quickly as possible."

"Time is money," she remarked.

Cooper checked his notes, then escorted Jayla to Mrs. Calvin's room and knocked on the door.

It was opened a few inches by an elderly toffee-skinned woman who squinted at them. A moment later, she threw the door open wide. "I was wondering when I'd see you again." She planted one hand on her hip and scowled at Cooper. "I hope you're here to tell me you caught the man who has been killing my tenants."

"Not quite yet," Cooper said, giving her an appealing, nearly helpless look. "That's why we came to ask for your help."

Mrs. Calvin's scowl was replaced with an indulgent smile. "Then I guess you'd both best come in. By the way, who is this? Don't tell me you got yourself married."

Cooper blushed, and Jayla felt her own face grow hot.

Mrs. Calvin laughed and patted her arm. "Don't you worry. I suppose you're some kind of special detective for the police or something. Or maybe one of those forensics specialists that were all over my house before. Come on in."

"This is Jayla Randall," Cooper told her as they followed her into the room and sat down on the couch. "She's a police dispatcher now, but last year she was taking 911 calls."

Mrs. Calvin's expression sobered. "Did you get the call from poor Jill?"

"Yes ma'am," Jayla said. "That was me."

"I'm sorry," Mrs. Calvin said, then smiled suddenly. "Would you like some coffee? I just made a fresh pot."

"That sounds great," Cooper said. "Thanks."

"Yes, thank you," Jayla said.

Mrs. Calvin poured them two cups, then sat down again. She addressed Jayla. "I don't know what he's told you about me, but I've rented out the apartments since my husband passed away twenty-two years ago. That killing last year was bad enough, but having another one as bad as the first? I've had more than enough. I'm moving to Florida so I can see my great-grandchildren grow up."

"I think that's a good idea," Cooper told her. "It's time you relax and enjoy yourself. You've earned it."

Mrs. Calvin gave him a playful swat on the back of the hand. "It's about time somebody took care of me, huh?"

"Exactly," he said. "How have things been here?"

"Nice and quiet," Mrs. Calvin said. "But I hate to leave Dallas. I've never lived anywhere else, but it's time for me to go. I couldn't stay on at my old place. There's no more happiness there for me."

"I can't blame you for leaving," Jayla said. Her heart went out to the old woman. "I wouldn't want to stay at that house either after all that's happened there."

"We wanted to see if there was anything you could tell us about the victims or what happened the nights they were murdered." Cooper removed his notepad and pen from his pocket. "Anything at all."

"No, I'm sorry," Mrs. Calvin said. "I already told you everything when I talked to you and Officer Stanley."

He remembered something he wanted to ask the landlady. "The last time we spoke, you mentioned that you used to have conversations with Katie sometimes. Did you ever talk with Jill?"

Mrs. Calvin considered the question. "No, Jill was always too busy to do much visiting with me."

Cooper was disappointed that Jill hadn't confided in Mrs. Calvin. "What about Mr. Peters? He worked for you, didn't he?"

Mrs. Calvin nodded. "For about five years. Maybe more. I'd have to check my records. He was always the nicest man. He kept the yard tidy and took care of all the little things in the house that needed fixing. He always saw to it that everything worked the way it should. And he'd call and check on me if we had a storm or anything."

Cooper jotted down notes. "That's good to hear."

"It sure is," Mrs. Calvin said. "When we had that big hailstorm a couple of years ago, you bet I was glad he came to check on us and fix the windows that got broken."

"Was Mr. Peters friends with any of your tenants?" he asked.

Mrs. Calvin considered for a moment. "I wouldn't say that, but he was always polite and willing to lend a hand. He'd help them if he saw them with packages or groceries. But there was nothing personal about it, nothing forward. He was kind and considerate." She shook her head. "I can't believe he would ever do something so terrible."

"What about when his wife died?" Jayla asked. "He must have been very upset."

"He was," Mrs. Calvin responded. "When he came to tell me, he sat at my kitchen table and cried like a baby. What could I do but give him a cup of coffee and listen to him? I don't hold with liquor, but I sure wished I had some that night. If ever a man needed something to cut the pain, it was him."

Jayla took a sip of her coffee. "Did he ever seem like he wasn't aware of where he was or what he was doing?"

Mrs. Calvin narrowed her eyes. "Do you mean confused or crazy?"

"Either one," Jayla said. "Maybe he said or did something that was out of character for him."

The older woman gave a derisive sniff. "He's nowhere near old enough for any of that. You young folk think anybody over fifty needs to be put out to pasture. I guess I should be locked up somewhere I can't hurt myself or wander off."

"Now don't go assuming things about the young either," Cooper told her with a wink. "I know you're as sharp as a box of scalpel blades. We're just trying to learn more about Mr. Peters."

Mrs. Calvin patted the iron-gray curls atop her head. "Well, to answer the question, I never saw him anything but in his right mind. In spite of all he's been through, he's a good, hardworking man I'd trust with my money and even my life."

"That says a lot about him," Cooper said gently. "But sometimes people aren't what they appear to be."

"Officer, I've been around a lot longer than you," Mrs. Calvin reminded him in a stern tone. "Don't you think I realize that?"

"I think you realize that I'm not with the police anymore too," he said.

"Officer, detective, whatever. You know what I mean, and don't act like you don't."

Cooper chuckled. "Do you have an address for Mr. Peters? I thought Jayla and I might stop by and see what else we can find out from his neighbors."

Mrs. Calvin tightened her jaw. "Are you trying to get him out of jail or keep him in?"

"We're trying to bring the truth to light," he said.

Jayla tilted her head, watching the woman's expression. "Do you do much gardening anymore?"

"Gardening? Me?" Mrs. Calvin's laugh was high and merry. "I never did when I could help it. I was born here in Dallas, but I still don't like the heat. No, Mr. Peters took care of the lawn and the flower beds. Before him, I had someone else. Why?"

Jayla shrugged. "I was wondering if you used any particular kind of gardening gloves."

"Don't keep any. Mr. Peters has all of that at his house. I don't want to see it or think about it. What kind of gloves?"

"They're for digging," Jayla said. "They have claws on the fingertips."

Mrs. Calvin made a face. "Claws? I've never seen any like that. Sounds kind of spooky."

"I think so too," Jayla admitted.

Mrs. Calvin went into the bedroom and got her purse. She took out a little notebook and pen and wrote something down. Then she handed the page to Cooper. "That's Mr. Peters's address. It's a couple of streets over from my house."

"I know where this is." Cooper drained his cup with a satisfied sigh, then set it on the table. "Thank you, ma'am." He gave her his card. "Will you call me before you leave town? I want to bring you some coffee."

"What for?" Mrs. Calvin asked.

"To make up for all the coffee you hand out to everybody who stops by your kitchen." He glanced around the elegant hotel room. "Wherever your kitchen may be."

"I wouldn't offer if I didn't like doing it," Mrs. Calvin said brusquely, but she seemed pleased all the same. "It's not much to do for folks, but it's at least a little way to share what blessings I have."

Jayla finished her own coffee and smiled at her. "Thank you for inviting us in. We're doing our best to figure out what happened. We both like Mr. Peters too, and we're trying to help him."

Mrs. Calvin patted her hand. "Bless you. The truth is what we all want."

"Everybody but the killer," Cooper said.

Mrs. Calvin took his arm and walked him toward the door. "You catch him, whoever it is. And you do it quick."

"I will," he promised.

Mrs. Calvin turned to Jayla, smiling again. "Watch out for this man," she whispered loudly, tapping her temple. "He doesn't always take care of himself, and he needs looking after."

"I'll do that," Jayla promised.

*If he'll let me.*

Jayla and Cooper left the hotel and drove to the duplex where Peters lived. It was a small, solidly built house, perfectly symmetrical, with the doors to each side on opposite ends of the covered porch. It looked as if it hadn't been significantly updated since it had been built, probably in the 1920s, but it was immaculately maintained, most likely by Peters.

Jayla checked the address Mrs. Calvin had given them. "He lives in the first unit," she said, pointing to the left side of the house.

"Then we'll go talk to Ray Jensen in the other one," Cooper told her.

They got out of the car and walked up to the door on the right.

Cooper rang the bell. "Pretty quiet out here," he observed, scanning the street behind them. "I guess we could knock on some neighbors' doors if we don't get an answer."

They waited, and he finally rang again.

"I'm coming," said a voice from inside, and then the door opened.

The man who answered was tall with white hair and sharp gray eyes. He was slightly stooped, but he didn't appear frail, despite the cane he leaned on. "Can I help you?"

"My name's Cooper Cole," he replied, offering his business card. "And this is Jayla Randall. Are you Ray Jensen?"

"Yes," he said. "What can I do for you?"

"If you have a minute, we'd like to talk to you," Cooper said.

The man's expression hardened. "About what?"

"We're trying to help Mr. Peters if we can," Jayla said. "I'm with the police, and Cooper is a private investigator. All we want is to talk to you for a few minutes."

Mr. Jensen seemed uncertain, and she couldn't blame him. There were too many people trying to take advantage of the elderly, and he'd likely been warned over and over again not to trust strangers.

"Can I see your badge?" Mr. Jensen asked Jayla.

"I have my ID." She dug it out of her purse, hoping that would do. "I'm not a police officer, but I do work for the department. Cooper was a policeman, but now he's a private investigator."

The man studied her photo, then her face.

Jayla almost hoped he wouldn't let them in, knowing how convincing some forgeries could be and how determined con artists were.

"Wait a minute," Mr. Jensen said. Keeping Jayla's ID, he closed the door and locked it.

"He's nobody's fool," Cooper said with a grin. "Good for him."

"I'm glad there's a covered porch," Jayla said, blotting the sweat off her upper lip with the back of one hand. It was already sweltering, and it wasn't even noon.

A few minutes later, Mr. Jensen came back to the door. "I called the police station and asked them about both of you. And I told them that if anything happened to me, they had your description and your license plate number."

Cooper couldn't quite hide a grin. "Nothing wrong with being careful."

He returned Jayla's ID. "Come on in."

It was deliciously cool inside, due in part to the whirring ceiling fan over the small living room. The place was simply furnished and mostly tidy apart from the plastic tub beside the recliner that contained numerous pill bottles, a blood pressure monitor, and a diabetic blood-testing kit. The large CD rack was full, and Jayla recognized a few titles from the big band era.

"Go ahead and sit down," Mr. Jensen said, sinking into a well-used chair.

Jayla and Cooper sat on the relatively new sofa across from the recliner.

"Now what's this about Daryl?" Mr. Jensen asked.

"It's about his arrest," Cooper began.

"Daryl was arrested?" Mr. Jensen sounded shocked.

"You didn't know?" Cooper asked.

"No, I had no idea," Mr. Jensen said. "I went out of town Friday morning. I just got home a few hours ago, and I found a note on my door asking me to call the police. That must be why."

"Have you contacted them yet?" Jayla asked.

"No, because it didn't say what it was about," Mr. Jensen answered. "I wanted my son to come over in case there was something I couldn't answer." He ran one hand over his white hair. "What happened?"

"Daryl was arrested for a murder committed last Thursday." Cooper told him about what had happened in the apartment and why Peters was arrested.

"No, no," Mr. Jensen said, sudden red patches in his withered cheeks. "Not Daryl. That's not him at all. He couldn't have done it."

"Why do you think that?" Cooper asked.

"Because he couldn't have. I can't sleep some nights, and my bedroom is right up against his on the other side of the house. I could hear him pacing and talking to himself like he usually does when he's troubled. It doesn't bother me. We all got problems, don't we?"

Jayla and Cooper both nodded.

"What do you think he might have been troubled about?" Jayla asked.

"His wife died a year ago," Mr. Jensen said. "I remember it was on the fifth because they always have the Cinco de Mayo parties and all that around town. Not that Daryl and his wife usually did anything special, but it stuck in my mind that she died that day. I suppose he was thinking of her. I lost my wife seventeen years ago, and I still struggle with missing her. I was seventy-six then. I didn't think I'd last so long without Edith."

"I'm sorry. It must be very difficult for you," Jayla said softly. "How did you get to know Daryl?"

"Oh, Edith and I lived here before he was born. We knew his folks and rented this place from them after the war."

Jayla knew he was referring to World War II. There was a faded black-and-white photograph of a young man in Navy dress blues among the others hanging on the wall behind him. She glimpsed traces of the young man in Mr. Jensen's eyes.

"We watched Daryl grow up, and we went to his wedding," Mr. Jensen continued. "We couldn't have kept living here if his folks hadn't held the rent down. Daryl did the same, and he's always checking on me and fixing things around the place so I don't have to call repairmen. My son is begging me to move, but I don't want to. Now if something happens to Daryl, I guess I'll have to."

"You're sure about what you heard?" Cooper asked. "And the date?"

"It was the night before I went on my trip. My great-granddaughter got married, and we went to the wedding in Houston." Mr. Jensen appeared faintly embarrassed. "I don't travel much anymore, and the trip really wore me out. You woke me up."

"Sorry," Cooper said.

"No, don't apologize," Mr. Jensen said. "This is a serious matter, and I want to help Daryl. What can I do?"

"When you get a chance, you need to tell your story to the police,"

Cooper said. "Actually, would it be better if someone came over to talk to you?"

Mr. Jensen nodded.

"I can call the officer in charge," Cooper said. "Officer Stanley. I'm sure he won't mind coming over."

"That would help a lot," Mr. Jensen admitted. "Like I said, I don't travel much anymore."

"No problem." Cooper took out his phone. "If you'll give me your phone number, I'll make sure Officer Stanley calls you to schedule a convenient time."

Mr. Jensen recited his number, and Cooper entered it into his phone.

"Do you remember what time it was when you couldn't sleep?" Jayla asked.

"As accurate as you can make it," Cooper added.

Mr. Jensen scratched one ear. "I don't know. I remember I fell asleep about eight, and when I woke up that show that follows real police calls was on. I watched three or four episodes of that before I fell asleep again."

Jayla noticed the large flat-screen TV mounted on the wall opposite from Mr. Jensen. "Do you have a television in your bedroom too?"

"Yes, it's a smaller one, but it works when I don't feel like getting up."

"Do you recall which episodes you happened to see?" Cooper asked. "I know they run that show pretty much all night."

The old man stroked his chin. "There was one that was in Fort Worth. I'm sure of that one because my niece's boy is a cop there. Seen that one a lot of times. There was another one that was in Las Vegas. No, maybe it was Phoenix. I couldn't say exactly, but I know what I heard, and I heard Daryl over there during the night."

Cooper smiled, but Jayla could see the disappointment in his eyes. "Anything else you remember?" he asked, getting to his feet.

"I guess I wasn't much help." Mr. Jensen clutched the handle of his cane. "I'm sorry."

Cooper clasped his shoulder. "It's fine. It's been almost a week since then, and you're tired."

Jayla got up too.

Mr. Jensen followed them to the front door. "Don't you let them railroad Daryl. I've known him all his life. He couldn't kill anybody. Not on purpose."

Jayla glanced at Cooper. Obviously, he'd noticed too.

"On purpose?" Cooper asked the older man.

"Daryl is not the kind of person to intentionally hurt someone else." Mr. Jensen frowned. "But I suppose anybody could do something accidentally. If he ever did anything like that—and I'm not saying he did—it wouldn't be on purpose."

"He comes off as a nice guy," Cooper said. "A good friend."

"He sure is. I won't believe anything bad about him."

Jayla stopped at the door. "I'm sure Daryl was upset when he lost his wife."

"Oh yes," Mr. Jensen said. "Very upset. I'd say he was depressed, but he got better after a few months."

"Did something happen that cheered him up?" Jayla asked.

"Not anything specific," Mr. Jensen said. "I think it was because of the holidays. Daryl and Marie always decorated the whole building to the nines for Christmas. I was afraid he was going to be too distraught to do it after she passed, but he came over and asked me what I thought about doing it all up again. He wanted to decorate the house so bright that Marie would be able to see it from heaven."

"What did you think of that?" Cooper asked.

"I thought it was the best thing he could do, and I helped as much as I could," Mr. Jensen told him. "He seemed better after that, and I felt better too. I hadn't put up anything since my Edith passed on."

"But what about now?" Cooper asked. "Before you went on your trip?"

Mr. Jensen shifted on his feet, leaning more heavily on his cane. "He was talking about his wife more than usual, probably because we were coming up on the anniversary of her passing. I could tell it still hurt him to remember her. I told him the pain wouldn't go away, but the good memories would be there too."

Jayla was sure there was the shimmer of tears in his eyes. She had to blink hard herself.

"Did he ever appear to be confused?" Cooper asked. "Like he didn't know where he was or anything?"

Mr. Jensen shook his head. "Daryl is as sound as a dollar. Not like me, always going into a room and forgetting why." He laughed.

Jayla smiled at him.

"Daryl told us that when his wife died, he didn't know where he was half the time," Cooper said. "What do you think he meant?"

Mr. Jensen scoffed. "That's grief. I'd have said the same thing when I lost Edith. Doesn't mean I walked around killing people. Questions like that are what's crazy."

"You're probably right," Cooper said. "Well, thanks for talking to us. I'll make sure Officer Stanley gets in touch with you."

"That'll be fine," Mr. Jensen said. He opened the front door, letting in the heat, the rumble of a lawn mower, and the smell of newly cut grass.

He shook his head. "It's too hot to be mowing, but people can take care of their own business. Of course, Daryl always took care of the lawn for us. Can't say what I'll do without him."

"We're going to do our best to find out what happened," Cooper said. "Don't you worry."

"I'll leave it to you then," Mr. Jensen said. "To both of you. You make a good team."

Jayla ducked her head.

"Between the two of us, we'll figure it out," Cooper said. "If anything else comes to mind, please call me."

Mr. Jensen held up the business card Cooper had given him. "I won't forget."

Jayla waited to speak until she and Cooper were back in the car and pulling away from the curb. "That didn't help much."

Cooper blew out his breath. "No, not really. For a minute there I thought he might be able to alibi Peters, but since he can't remember exactly when he heard him, that won't work."

"What about when he said Peters wouldn't kill somebody *on purpose*?"

"Hard to say." He paused. "It could be exactly what he said, that he's just not the type to murder anyone. Or it could mean that he has a few doubts about his neighbor's mental state after his wife died. I don't know."

"Unless Peters had that psychotic break we talked about and didn't realize what he was doing," Jayla suggested.

"It's possible," Cooper admitted. "He doesn't strike me as the type, but Stanley says they'll check him out."

"Poor guy. Even if Peters did it, I feel bad for him."

"It's tough on him either way. For now, I'll get in touch with the station that runs those police shows. They should be able to tell me what time they ran the one he remembers so clearly."

"I hope it helps," she said. But she didn't feel any more hopeful than he sounded. Unless they could discover exactly what time that Fort Worth episode had aired, the only one Mr. Jensen was sure he remembered, the information wouldn't have any bearing. What he had heard from the other side of the duplex could have taken place well before the murder or well after it.

If the person he had heard had been Daryl Peters at all.

"Call Stanley," Cooper ordered the hands-free system, and the phone began to ring.

"Stanley," the brusque voice answered a moment later. "Is this Cooper?"

"Yeah. We talked to Daryl Peters's next-door neighbor. Well, the guy on the other side of the duplex. Ray Jensen is sure Peters was home the night of the Myers murder."

"How can he be sure?"

"He claims he heard him in the duplex at the time," Cooper said.

"You believe him?"

"I believe he's telling the truth, but I can't say whether that proves anything." Cooper glanced at Jayla. He could see it in her eyes that she wanted him to clear Peters, but he couldn't do it. Not yet.

"What do you mean?" Stanley asked.

Cooper told him what Mr. Jensen had said about the police show he watched and how that may or may not hold any weight. "But I'm going to see if I can track down which episodes were on that night and exactly what times they aired."

"Sounds good."

"Meanwhile, you need to visit Mr. Jensen and get his statement," Cooper continued. "He's ninety-three, so he'd appreciate it if he didn't have to travel to the station. He really wants to help clear Peters."

"Enough to lie for him?" Stanley asked.

Cooper considered. "He doesn't come across that way, but I never met the guy before today. It's possible that he's simply a good actor. Peters and his family have treated him well. Maybe he thinks he owes him something."

"What's the neighbor's name again?" Stanley asked. "Hang on. I'll write it down."

Cooper gave him Jensen's first and last names and his phone number. "He's in the second unit of Peters's duplex."

"Okay, I'll call him up and then get his statement," Stanley said. "Anything else I need to be aware of?"

"No," Cooper said. "Any word on that psych exam scheduled for Daryl?"

"Not yet. Why?"

Cooper filled him in on what Mr. Jensen had said about Peters not killing anybody on purpose.

"Yeah," Stanley said. "I'll put that in the file and let the psychiatrists know."

"Good. You got anything new?"

"I do," Stanley said, "so what this Jensen says might be a moot point."

"You mean about the DNA under Katie Myers's fingernails?"

Stanley sighed. "Your brother has a big mouth."

Jayla put her hand over her mouth, smothering a giggle.

"I was going to hear about it anyway," Cooper said. "I thought we'd all do better if we shared what we learn."

"Okay, as long as the city doesn't have to pick up your bill."

"Nope," Cooper said. "I know you can't get blood from a turnip."

"Very funny," Stanley said. "Still, keep in mind that anything you get from us can't go anywhere else. Do you understand?"

"Yes I do."

"Not even to your client," Stanley added.

"I promise," Cooper said. "I told her I wanted to find the truth, but I'm still the main witness against her husband. She's paying me, but she didn't buy me, okay?"

"All right, you keep it that way," Stanley said. "I'll go see this neighbor. You keep your nose clean."

"Yes sir," Cooper said.

"Talk to you later." Stanley hung up.

Cooper glanced at Jayla. "So what now? You ready to go home?"

"I guess I should," she replied. "I have stuff to do. What about you?"

"I'd better call Laurel and tell her about our conversation with Mr. Jensen," he said. "She's counting on Peters being the one responsible for both murders."

"She's not going to be happy about that," Jayla said.

"No, but I didn't promise I'd clear her husband," Cooper said. "I told her that I'd try to figure out what actually happened. She can always fire me and get somebody else if she doesn't like what I discover."

He steered toward Jayla's place, feeling her eyes on him.

"Would you mind calling Laurel while I'm with you?" Jayla asked.

"I don't know why not," Cooper answered. "Do you want to talk to her?"

"No, I just thought it might be helpful to hear what she has to say firsthand. Sometimes how people say things is as important as what they say."

He raised his eyebrows. "Woman's intuition?"

She gave him a sly smile.

Cooper returned his attention to the road. He could get used to having Jayla with him. No, he should have thought of that before he broke up with her. If he could solve this case, maybe he could sort out his own feelings enough to decide what to do about Jayla.

"Okay, sure," he said. "I'll call her next. If you really want her to be herself, don't let her know you're here. Women are different around other women than they are around men."

"Only her kind of woman," Jayla said.

Cooper chuckled and pulled into the empty parking lot of a comedy club, then called Laurel's number.

She answered immediately. "I was hoping it would be you. You must have news if you're calling me already."

"Yes I do," he said. "I talked to Daryl Peters's neighbor, and he claims Peters was home the night Katie Myers was murdered."

"Can he prove it?" Laurel asked.

"He said he heard Peters on his side of the duplex."

"And he can verify the exact time?" Laurel pressed.

"I'm not positive about that," Cooper answered. "We're checking into it. He's an elderly gentleman, and we want to make sure he's got his facts straight."

Laurel huffed. "Are you saying this man is senile?"

"No, not at all," he responded. "We simply want to verify everything before we make any kind of conclusions."

"I suppose by 'we' you mean the woman you're working with."

Cooper gave Jayla a wink. "There's the police too. We all have the same objective, and that's to uncover what actually happened. Like you, I want to dig up as much as I can about everyone involved in the case, including the suspect, witness, and any interested parties."

"I think that's wise."

"We know where your husband was when the second murder was committed," he said.

"I don't think even the DA has any doubts about that."

"What about you?" Cooper asked. "What were you doing at the time?"

"I was at home asleep, if you must know." Laurel definitely sounded put out. "And no, there was no one with me."

"I didn't mean to imply there would be. Not with your husband still in custody. I suppose you have staff members who would have seen you that night."

"Yes. My housekeeper lives in. She brought me a cup of hot chocolate when I couldn't get to sleep that night. Earlier in the day, I went to the groundbreaking ceremony at the new center for disadvantaged children the Wolff Foundation is building. Afterward the whole team responsible for bringing it together came over for dinner and cocktails. They ended up staying until nearly eight."

"Sounds like a nice party," he said.

"Then I was on a conference call with my banker and the head of the foundation about several financial issues that came up during dinner," Laurel went on, ignoring his remark. "It lasted almost two hours. After that I was exhausted."

"But you couldn't sleep," Cooper said.

Jayla rolled her eyes.

"You know how it is," Laurel told him with a sigh. "I had my housekeeper call my masseuse and have her come over. Then I spent an hour in the Jacuzzi listening to nature sounds while I soaked. It didn't do a bit of good."

"I'm sorry," Cooper murmured, wanting to laugh but wondering if she was laying it on a little too thick. "What time was the groundbreaking ceremony?"

"Three thirty. I was almost late. I was thinking all day that it was at four, but fortunately my housekeeper reminded me."

"How long did the ceremony last?"

"About forty-five minutes," Laurel replied. "We had a statement by the head of the foundation about our purpose for the center, and he thanked everyone who had contributed to it. Many of Dallas's leading citizens have been very generous. After that, the mayor said a few words and was kind enough to remember several things the foundation has done in the needier parts of the city. Following that was the actual groundbreaking ceremony."

"Were you the one with the shovel?"

"I was. It was spray-painted gold. There were cameras and reporters everywhere, and we were on the news on several local channels. Did you see any of the coverage?"

"No, I usually don't have much time for TV," Cooper said. "But I'm sure the exposure will be a lot of help for your foundation."

"Exactly," Laurel said. "It's not about me. It's about awareness. Donations are flooding in." There was a touch of self-consciousness in her soft laugh. "Of course, not having Dane with me on such an important occasion was difficult, but you know how long this case has taken already. We didn't feel right about keeping the children waiting for the center to be built simply because he has been unfairly charged. And Dane wouldn't hear of postponing it any longer."

"Sounds like you took care of everything just fine," he commented.

"I think he'd be pleased. But he'd be much more pleased if you'd found definite evidence that Daryl Peters is guilty. If he's not, what are you going to do next?"

"I'm not sure yet," Cooper admitted. "I'm going to track down that 911 recording and see where that leads me. Peters is far from cleared at this point. But with the neighbor's testimony, the case against him might break down pretty fast."

"But the evidence—"

"Is kind of bizarre," he said, interrupting her. "He could be telling the truth about how he was scratched."

"But wouldn't his DNA be on the woman's body?"

"True," Cooper said, "but it could also have been planted there."

She gave a barely audible gasp. "Really?"

"Lots of things are possible. We'll have to wait until forensics finishes their report."

He remembered Kelly saying there had been an attempt to wash the victim's hands. It was possible that it was a clumsy way to explain why the physical evidence didn't look the way it should have if Katie Myers had really struggled with Peters.

"What happens if he is cleared?" Laurel asked.

"I'll see what else I can find out," Cooper said. "Is there anyone else you suspect could be involved?"

"I don't know. Dane said Jill had a boyfriend."

"Do the police know about this man?"

"We both mentioned it to the police at the time," Laurel said.

Jayla raised her eyebrows and stared at Cooper.

"What did the police say?" Cooper asked.

"They brushed it off because they were certain that Dane was guilty."

"What did Dane say about him?" he asked.

"Dane mentioned this other man was the reason why he broke things off with her," Laurel said. "Though that was really the last straw. I told him she was using him for the money, and once he heard about this guy, he finally believed me."

"Do you have any information about him?" Cooper added, getting a notepad and pen from the cup holder. "Name? Address? Description?"

"Let me think what his name was." After a few seconds of silence, she said, "It was Evan or Eric or something like that. I can ask Dane what he remembers. I'm sure he said the guy managed one of the bands that played in Deep Ellum. But I don't know what kind of music. He mentioned that he was a big guy and his arms were heavily tattooed."

Cooper jotted down the information. "Do you remember the name of the band? What specific clubs they played? Anything like that?"

"No, I'll have to ask Dane. I'm not sure what he actually knows anyway. I think he discovered a picture of this man in Jill's phone, and they had a big fight over it."

"Can you tell me anything else?"

"I think part of the blowup between her and my husband was because he got into her phone without telling her and erased a lot of pictures of her and other men. But Dane and I talked about that more than a year ago. I don't remember too many details."

"What did the police turn up on him?"

"I don't think they ever seriously searched for him, but maybe he was the one who killed her. If Daryl Peters didn't do it, then who else would?"

"Let's suppose Jill's boyfriend is the only one who'd have a reason to kill her," Cooper said. "Why would this particular guy have killed Katie Myers the other night?"

"I don't know," Laurel said, frustration evident in her voice. "Maybe he went crazy when he killed that woman last year and feels like he has to do it every year. Dane is the first to admit that he has made mistakes, but he didn't kill her. You can't stand by and let him be convicted, possibly even given the death penalty, for something he didn't do."

No, Cooper couldn't. And he'd heard of cases and even been involved in cases where the evidence was stronger than this and the accused was eventually proven innocent. Perhaps he was the right man for the job. Not for Laurel or her husband. Not even for the sake of truth and justice. Just so he could sleep at night after he testified at Wolff's trial.

Laurel didn't say anything else, but he could hear her slight, trembling breaths.

"How am I supposed to track down this mystery man?" Cooper asked heavily.

"You're the detective," Laurel snapped. "I told you everything Dane told me about him. What do you want me to say?"

It made sense. If the man was seeing Jill in the apartment Dane was paying for, he wouldn't exactly want to hang around when Dane was likely to be there.

Cooper didn't remember hearing about this guy before, but maybe it had been such a minor thing that he'd overlooked it. Or forgotten it. His blood ran cold. What else might he have forgotten over the past year?

"I'll see what I can find out," he said. "Anything else?"

"No, nothing. But I'll talk to Dane and get back to you if he remembers anything more than what I told you."

"Thank you. I'll be waiting to hear from you." Cooper ended the call and faced Jayla. "Well?"

"I've never heard a bigger phony," Jayla said.

"You think Laurel's a phony?" Cooper asked.

Jayla nodded. "I'm not saying that what she told you isn't true, but she certainly has a high opinion of herself."

He grinned. "Why shouldn't she?"

She rolled her eyes.

"No, I'm serious. She's beautiful, intelligent, stylish, connected, and she's exactly the kind of wife you'd expect Dane Wolff to have. But I agree that she's a phony."

"But not necessarily lying."

"No, not necessarily," Cooper said, pulling back onto the street. "What did you think about Jill's mysterious boyfriend?"

Jayla shrugged. "It sounds like a logical reason for Dane to end his relationship with Jill."

"It does," he said, "but I don't remember anything about a boyfriend in Laurel's statement or her husband's."

Jayla sat up straighter in her seat. It wasn't like him to miss something important. "Is this the first time you've heard about him?"

"I'm not sure," Cooper admitted. "It's possible that it was only a mention, and I missed it. But at least she gave me some information about this guy, so I have somewhere to start."

"Wolff should be able to tell his wife even more about him. Or maybe you should talk to him directly."

"It might get to that," he said. "We'll see what she comes up with first."

"Have you ever talked to him?"

Cooper shook his head. "I always figured he was the guy, and if he wasn't, then the department would work that out. But . . ."

"Now you're not so sure," Jayla said.

"I want to make sure. I'm going to talk to Stanley again about the statements they have from Wolff and his wife and see if he remembers them saying anything about the boyfriend. First I'll take you home."

"You aren't taking me with you?" she asked with a touch of a smile, hoping she sounded interested and not needy.

"You said you had things to do," he reminded her.

"I'd rather learn the truth about the statements."

"That's fine with me. I'll call Stanley and ask if he's got a minute to talk to us about the case and if he'll let us peek at that part of the evidence." Cooper pulled into a parking lot and called Stanley.

"You again?" Stanley asked as soon as he answered. "Can't you give a guy a break?"

Cooper chuckled. "Sorry. I was hoping you'd be at the station so we could talk about the Kinner and Myers cases."

"Is it urgent?" Stanley asked.

"No. When's a better time for you?"

"What about tomorrow?" Stanley asked. "Unless something comes up, I should be around all day."

"That should work," Cooper answered. "We'll see you then." He disconnected, then faced Jayla. "How about I take you home? We'll get back on the case tomorrow morning. I'll pick you up at nine. Fair enough?"

"Fine with me," she said.

"If you think of anything else, give me a call, all right? It doesn't matter what time it is."

"I promise, but I don't know if I'll ever be able to remember."

That night Jayla did remember.

As she tossed and turned in her bed, the sounds from the 911 call replayed in her head, accompanied by the terrible images that had flooded her mind while she heard them. Without anything but the audio of the scene, she had conjured up the images out of her own deepest fears. Before last week, they had faded to a bearable level. But tonight they were vivid again, coming to her the moment she tried to drop off to sleep, making her jerk awake over and over until she was finally too exhausted to think anymore.

Then her telephone jolted her. Jayla didn't recognize the number and considered not answering, but maybe it was an emergency. She was wide-awake anyway.

"Hello?" she croaked, then cleared her dry throat and tried again. "Hello?"

Silence.

Jayla held her breath, her hand shaking as she pressed the phone to her ear, waiting. Someone was listening, waiting for her to speak. But she refused to make a sound. Somehow she knew the person on the other end was a man.

"Jayla." The voice was indistinct, not exactly a whisper but almost too low to hear, and there was something about it that turned her blood cold.

The phone shook in her hands, and she clenched her jaw to keep her teeth from chattering. She wouldn't scream.

"You know who this is."

Yes, Jayla knew. It was the same low, guttural voice she'd heard on that 911 call last year. She tried to block it out. She wanted to hang up, but she couldn't move.

"You remember me," the voice hissed. "And I remember you." He paused.

She imagined he was waiting for her to respond. He most likely wanted her to scream, plead with him to leave her alone, or cry. But she held perfectly still and didn't utter a sound.

"Now you'd better forget," he said. "Forget everything." Finally, there was a click and then a dial tone.

Jayla switched off her phone, tossed it into her purse, and carried her purse out to the living room and left it on the couch. Then she made herself a pot of coffee.

She wouldn't be sleeping again.

Even though Jayla had resigned to stay up the rest of the night, she ended up dozing off sometime during the night.

The alarm startled her awake the next morning. Her heart thundered in her chest as the eerie phone call resurfaced in her mind. Had it been the same voice from the 911 call last year? Had Jayla really talked to the murderer? It seemed impossible, yet she couldn't imagine who else it could have been. However, the man never mentioned either murder, so maybe it wasn't the killer.

Feeling groggy, Jayla struggled out of bed and put on a new pot of coffee. As she got ready to go to the police station with Cooper, she waffled over the identity of the caller. The only thing that remained constant was the fear that had settled into her bones after hearing the man's terrifying voice.

After drinking a cup of coffee and eating a light breakfast of fruit and yogurt, Jayla headed to the living room to wait for Cooper.

Mary Ann joined her. "Where are you going?"

"To the station with Cooper."

"That figures." Mary Ann crossed her arms over her chest. "I don't think it's a good idea to get so involved with him or this murder case."

"I feel like it's my responsibility to do what I can to help," Jayla said, her voice cracking. "I don't want anyone else to get killed."

"I know," Mary Ann said, giving Jayla a hug. "You have such a big heart." When Mary Ann pulled away, she looked at her sister and frowned. "What's wrong?"

Jayla was a nervous wreck about the phone call last night, but she didn't want to tell Mary Ann. It wouldn't do any good to frighten her. "Maybe you should stay with Mom and Dad."

"Why?"

Jayla shrugged, trying to act nonchalant. "It might do you some good to get away for a few days."

"I'm not going anywhere," Mary Ann said. "I know you're upset about everything that's been going on, and I don't want to leave you here alone."

Before Jayla could argue, there was a knock on the door.

With a scowl, Mary Ann marched back to her room.

Still feeling rattled, Jayla took a deep breath and opened the door.

Cooper studied her. "Are you okay?"

"Just tired. I didn't get much sleep." She pasted on a smile and grabbed her purse. "I'm ready to go."

As he escorted her to the car, he kept stealing glances at her.

Once they were settled inside, Cooper started the car, then turned to Jayla. "Something's going on. Please tell me."

She needed to inform Stanley about the phone call last night, and she might as well let Cooper know first. There was no need to have them both going crazy at the same time.

Jayla touched Cooper's arm. "I got a call at about three o'clock this morning," she said, her throat suddenly dry. "I believe it was from the same man on the 911 tape."

He set his jaw. "What did he say to you?"

"He didn't speak at first, but I could tell he was listening." She shivered. "Then he said my name."

"What did you do?"

"I wasn't going to give him the satisfaction of getting upset," Jayla continued. "I waited for him to talk. Finally, he said, 'You know who this is. You remember me. And I remember you.'" She swallowed the lump in her throat. "Then he said I'd better forget everything."

Cooper reached over and took her hand. "How sure are you that it was the same man as on the 911 call last year?"

She thought for a moment. "I've been trying to figure it out ever since he called. I'm not absolutely sure, but I think so. His voice sounded familiar." Her heartbeat sped up at the memory.

"Did he say anything specific to the murders?"

"No, and that's another reason why I can't be completely sure it was the same man," Jayla answered. "It's been a year since I heard his voice. I wish I could listen to the tape of that call from the night Jill was murdered. I might be able to tell if it's the same guy."

"Are you sure that was all he said?" he asked. "No threats? No obscenities? No taunting?"

"Nothing like that. He said I remembered him and he remembered me and that I should forget everything." She shuddered. "Who else would say that besides the murderer?"

"Did the phone number come up on your caller ID?"

"Yes. The area code was local," Jayla replied. "It's still in the call list on my phone."

"But not a number you recognized?" Cooper persisted.

She shook her head.

"So it couldn't have been Daryl Peters."

"If he'd called from the jail, it would have been collect," Jayla said. "There also would have been a recording saying it was from the prison and asking if I wanted to accept, but it was a regular call."

"And the same would apply to Dane," he reasoned.

She nodded, not liking his implication that the killer was still at large.

"Are you okay?" Cooper asked, squeezing her hand.

"I'm fine," she said. And it was true. But only in the light of day when Cooper was holding her hand.

"Are you sure?" he asked, studying her. "Why didn't you tell me right away?"

"I didn't want to wake you up in the middle of the night," Jayla replied.

"I told you to call me anytime," Cooper reminded her.

"I was frightened, but nothing actually happened. I didn't want you to think I couldn't handle something like that on my own."

"Did you report it?"

"No, but I thought now would be a good time."

He shook his head, his mouth in a hard line. "You should have reported it immediately. It could be part of the Myers case."

"I know, and I'm sorry," Jayla said. "I'll tell Stanley when we get to the station. But ask him about Jill's boyfriend first. I don't want this to be all about me."

"Okay, let's go." Cooper released her hand, then shifted the car into gear and pulled away from the curb.

They were quiet during the short drive. Jayla felt anxious. She dreaded telling Stanley about the phone call. It had been hard enough describing it to Cooper.

When Jayla and Cooper arrived at the station, they ran into Kelly coming off duty. He approached them with a broad grin. "Who's this? She seems familiar."

"Cut it out," Jayla said, blushing. "How are you? How's Jen?"

Kelly gave her a hug. "We're both good. Jen told me to invite you over for dinner the next time I ran into you at the station. So what do you say?"

"When?" she asked.

"Cooper's coming on Saturday night for lasagna," Kelly answered. "You could come then."

"I am?" Cooper asked, blinking at his brother.

"You said name the day, so I'm naming it," Kelly replied, then returned his attention to Jayla. "Will you join us?"

"I'll have to check my schedule," Jayla hedged. She glanced at Cooper, wanting some kind of sign from him about whether or not he wanted her to accept the invitation. The last thing she needed was to make things awkward with him.

"You're free," Kelly said. "I mean, you're not scheduled to work." He grinned at her. "I already checked."

"I'm game if you are," Cooper told Jayla. "You can't do any better than Jen's lasagna and garlic bread."

"That's so true," Jayla said. "Okay, I'll be there. But no Scrabble. I'm tired of losing every time."

Kelly held up his hand. "No Scrabble, I promise. How about Twister?"

Jayla laughed. "No way. Go home and tell Jen to call me if she wants me to bring anything."

Kelly leaned closer to her and whispered conspiratorially, "Don't tell Jen I said this because she'll think I'm being rude, but if you happened to make your special fudge cake and brought it along, I wouldn't object."

"Me either," Cooper said, "and don't expect there to be much left by the end of the night."

"Deal," Jayla said with a smile. "What time should I arrive?"

"How's seven?" Kelly asked.

"Sounds good," Jayla said.

"Great. See you both then." Kelly started down the hall.

"Hey!" Cooper called after him.

Kelly came back. "Yeah?"

"Have you been through the statements on the Kinner case?"

Kelly frowned. "No. I've heard Stanley and some of the others talk about it, but it's not something I've had anything to do with. Why?"

"Have you heard anyone mention her having a boyfriend?" Cooper asked. "I mean, besides Wolff."

Kelly shook his head.

"Nobody ever said anything about a guy named Eric or Evan?" Cooper continued. "He's a big guy with tattoos, and he manages a band."

"Not that I heard, but I never really went digging for it," Kelly said. "Why do you ask?"

"Laurel says this guy is the reason her husband ended his relationship with Jill. She wants me to find the guy and see if he could have killed Jill or Katie."

"That's news to me," Kelly said. "You should talk to Stanley. He's the expert. Or you could ask Kent or Daniels. They've been working on the case too. They might have checked into some of that old stuff."

Cooper nodded. "Are any of them here? Stanley mentioned he'd be around all day, but something always seems to come up."

"I don't know," Kelly said. "Ask Sheila. She knows everything about everybody."

"True," Cooper said with a chuckle. "All right. We'll see you Saturday. Tell Jen I said hi."

"Will do," Kelly said. He smiled at Jayla. "Good to see you again."

Jayla watched him until he turned a corner and was gone. "I've missed seeing him and Jen," she said finally.

"They've missed you too," Cooper said. "I hadn't even thought about things from their perspective."

"You can't date somebody just because it makes your family happy."

"But you still could have spent time with them," he said. "They didn't stop being your friends."

"It would have been weird." She raised her chin. "I didn't want them to feel sorry for me."

"They like you for yourself," Cooper insisted. "They always did. Not because they feel sorry for you. The one they should feel sorry for is me. For being such a fool."

Jayla didn't dare ask him what he meant by that remark. As much as she would have liked to, she didn't want to assume he was referring to breaking up with her.

"Come on. Let's talk to Sheila." Cooper ushered her to the front desk. "How are you doing?" he asked the receptionist.

Sheila batted her eyelashes at him. "Much better now that you're here." She reached over and patted Jayla's arm. "How are you?"

"I'm doing fine," Jayla said, even though she was still shaken. "How's Max?"

Sheila sighed. "Not any better. There's a treatment the doctors want to try, but our insurance company won't pay for it."

"Oh, I'm sorry," Jayla said, wishing she could do something to help. "We should have a fundraiser here at the station. Everyone loves you, and I'm sure they'd be glad to pitch in."

Sheila fiddled with a pen holder on her desk. "Thanks. We're still fighting with the insurance company, but maybe they'll change their mind." She folded her hands on the desk. "So what can I do for you two?"

"We're looking for Stanley," Cooper said. "Have you seen him lately?"

"I'm sure he's around somewhere. Hang on." Sheila picked up her phone and dialed. "Hey, is Stanley over there?" She paused. "Okay, don't let him leave. He's got company."

Sheila directed Jayla and Cooper to one of the interrogation rooms on the far side of the building.

"How are you holding up?" Cooper whispered as he escorted her down the hall.

"I'm okay." Jayla managed a slight smile, but her stomach was churning.

Though she wanted to know if the man who had called her last night was the murderer, she was afraid to discover the truth. It was terrifying that the man had her phone number. What else did he know about her?

And how far would he go to keep her quiet?

When Cooper and Jayla arrived at the interrogation room Sheila had told them about, Stanley was walking out the door.

"What's up?" Stanley asked, stuffing papers into a folder.

"Got a minute?" Cooper asked, giving Jayla a sidelong glance.

"A short minute," Stanley said. "Today has been more hectic than I expected. What's wrong?"

"Nothing's wrong," Cooper said. "I still need to ask you that question about the Kinner case."

Stanley frowned at one of the papers in his hand, then stuck it into the folder with the others. "Shoot."

"Do you remember Wolff or his wife saying anything about Jill having a boyfriend other than him?" Cooper asked.

"No," Stanley said. "Why?"

"Laurel mentioned Jill's other boyfriend a couple of times. She says if Peters didn't kill Jill, then maybe it was the other guy. I was wondering if you remember her or her husband saying that in their statements last year."

"I don't remember that, but it's been a long time." Stanley held up his folder. "I've had a lot going on. Do you know anything else about this guy?"

"Laurel said his name is Eric or Evan," Cooper replied. "He's a big man with a lot of tattoos, and he manages a band in Deep Ellum."

"That's not very much to go on," Stanley remarked.

"Laurel promised to ask her husband for any details he remembers and get back to me," Cooper said.

Stanley nodded.

"Do you mind if we check their statements?" Cooper asked. "I'd like to know exactly what was said about the guy back then."

"Wouldn't that have been part of the investigation if they'd brought it up at the time?" Jayla asked.

"It should have been," Stanley said.

"That's what I thought too," Cooper said. "Laurel claimed she mentioned it, but the cops brushed it off because they were certain that Dane was guilty."

Stanley snorted. "His attorneys should have said something if that's the case. They kicked up a fuss at the time about Daryl Peters being the one. Come on, you two. I want to read those statements myself."

He walked fast when he was annoyed, and Cooper and Jayla scrambled to keep up with him. It took him only a few minutes to get copies of the statements Wolff and his wife had made over the course of the investigation.

"Let's go to my office," Stanley suggested, leading the way.

Inside his office, Stanley sat down at his desk and motioned to the guest chairs facing him.

Cooper and Jayla took their seats.

Stanley began reading one of the papers. "Both Wolff and his wife claimed that Jill Kinner had a boyfriend and—" He broke off, frowning. "I don't remember this part at all." He slid the paper across the desk.

Cooper realized it was a transcript of Wolff's statement.

*I don't know anything except Jill called him Eric. He managed one of the bands that played locally. I saw a picture of the two of them on her phone. He appeared to be around thirty-five. He had long, dark hair. Dark eyes, brown or black. Tattoos on both arms. I think he hit her sometimes, but*

*she never told me that. I don't know where he lives. Maybe
he was mad at her for dating me. But there was also Daryl
Peters, the maintenance man at the apartment building.*

It was there in the very middle where the detective was asking
Wolff who he thought could have killed Jill Kinner. He went on to
talk about Peters after that.

Cooper handed the page to Jayla.

"This is the wife's statement," Stanley said, giving Cooper
another page.

*What about her boyfriend? Dane says he's been violent
with her. That's probably why she left him in the first place.
I don't know why she would want to go back.*

"That's all they said about the guy, as far as mentioning him as a
suspect," Stanley said. "But why don't I remember that?"

"Wolff's attorneys didn't follow up on this Eric guy?" Jayla asked.
"Not even at the beginning of the case?"

"Not that I heard," Stanley said.

"Did Jill ever file a complaint against Eric?" Cooper scanned the
papers again. "Against anybody for domestic violence?"

"She didn't." Stanley shuffled through more papers. "It was one of
the things the prosecution had against Wolff. She never filed a report,
but she was in the ER a couple of times for cracked ribs, a split lip,
and a broken nose. She always happened to fall down the stairs or trip
over something."

Cooper clenched his jaw as he read that part of the report. "And
this was while Jill was with Wolff? I mean, when she was living in
the apartment?"

Stanley nodded.

Jayla took the paper and read it. "Maybe Eric was responsible for Jill's injuries. He could have been furious with her for being with Wolff."

"Then why was she still seeing him?" Cooper asked. "Eric, I mean. If she wasn't seeing Eric again, why was Wolff mad enough to break things off with her?"

Jayla handed him the papers. "Maybe it was an excuse. If Wolff wanted to work things out with his wife and he didn't want to tell Jill, he could have claimed she was cheating on him and that was why he was dumping her."

"But if Eric was the one beating her up, wouldn't Wolff have said something, even if he only suspected it?" Stanley asked. "If she wouldn't press charges, wouldn't Wolff have tried to get the police to do something?"

"Possibly not," Jayla said. "Jill probably told Wolff the same story she told the hospital about falling or whatever, though it doesn't look like Wolff believed her. Maybe she thought she was keeping him and Eric from fighting, even keeping one of them from getting killed."

"It's hard to say in these domestic violence cases," Stanley said.

"Is there anything in the file that talks about the police searching for Eric?" Jayla asked.

Stanley shook his head. "Not that I know of."

"Somebody should have at least asked around some of the clubs," Cooper said. "If he was managing a band, somebody had to know him."

"I don't remember Wolff or his wife talking about the guy," Stanley said.

"Will you have somebody investigate it now?" Jayla asked. "It seems to be important for both cases."

"Yeah, you're right," Stanley said. "I'll definitely have one of my men see what he can find out."

"We'll check into it too," Cooper offered. "I have a friend who's been playing in Deep Ellum for a long time. He should have heard of this Eric guy. Maybe he has a last name or something else we can go on."

"Good," Stanley said. "Get back to me on that."

"I will." Cooper glanced at Jayla. "But there's something else we need to tell you about."

"What is it?" Stanley asked.

"I got a phone call in the middle of the night," she said.

"A phone call?" Stanley repeated, leaning forward.

"I think the call was from the man who killed Jill Kinner," Jayla said. Stanley grabbed a notepad and a pen. "Tell me exactly what happened."

She gave her statement and answered Stanley's questions.

Cooper had already asked her the same ones. He knew her answers could have bearing on both the Kinner and the Myers cases.

"If the man calls you again, do you think you could talk to him?" Stanley asked her once she had finished the report.

"What do you mean?" Jayla asked, her voice rising in pitch.

"If you talked to whoever's calling you, he might say something that would give us a clue," Stanley suggested.

Cooper frowned. "What if he says something and then realizes he's given himself away? Then he'll have to get rid of Jayla."

"I'll assign a couple of officers to watch her house," Stanley said.

"For how long? A day or two?" Cooper's frown deepened. He knew that the department didn't have the budget to watch Jayla's house for an extended period of time. "Until something else has priority?"

"Come on," Stanley said. "We'll do what we can."

"Why would he call me back anyway?" Jayla asked.

"You were the one who overheard the first murder," Stanley said. "Whether or not you actually recognize his voice, he might think you do. I'm guessing he wants to scare you into not testifying."

"But it couldn't have been Wolff," she protested. "He's still in jail."

"A copycat might have called you, trying to sound like Wolff," Stanley reasoned. "He might want to see if he can get the same kind of thrill by giving you a good scare."

Jayla gripped the armrests. "I don't like the fact he has my number."

"I don't either," Cooper said. "It's too easy for people to get that information these days."

"So, what do you say?" Stanley asked her. "Are you up for it?"

She nodded. "If I hear from him again, I'll give it a try, but I doubt I'll be able to ask him very much."

"I want you to tell somebody that he called," Cooper said. "And I mean immediately."

"Okay." Jayla turned to Stanley. "Are we done talking about this?"

"All done," he assured her.

"Have you discovered anything new on the Myers case?" Cooper asked him.

"Not yet," Stanley said. "How about you?"

"I'm working on it," Cooper replied. "I'll make sure to tell you about it if I come up with anything."

"Sounds good," Stanley said.

"One other thing," Cooper added. "Laurel hired me to discover what I can about both murders in the apartment. I thought you'd like to know."

Stanley didn't appear pleased. "All right, but make sure you do what you said and copy me on anything you learn."

"Got it."

Stanley gathered all the papers from the Kinner case and stuffed them into the folder. "I'll get these back where they belong." He held up the other folder he'd brought with him from the interrogation room. "Then I have to get someone assigned to my other case before

I can return to Myers and Kinner. You two keep me posted. And stay out of trouble." With that, he strode down the hallway and was gone.

"Are you ready to go?" Cooper asked.

Jayla nodded.

They left the room and waved goodbye to Sheila on the way out the door.

As they walked to his car, Jayla kept glancing at him.

Cooper wanted to say something to her, but he didn't know how.

"What?" she asked once they were both settled inside the car and buckled in.

"Nothing," he said as he pulled out of the parking lot. "Why?"

"You definitely have something on your mind."

"I was thinking about Daryl Peters again."

"Would it do any good for me to talk to him again?" Jayla asked.

Cooper studied her face for a moment before returning his attention to the road. "I know you didn't like talking to him before, and I understand."

"It might be helpful to listen to him," she said. "Just to make sure he's not the one who called me."

"How could Peters have done it?" he asked. "You said yourself he would have had to call collect, and you'd have gotten a recording saying the call was coming from the jail."

"But maybe he had somebody help him get around that." She paused. "What if he called somebody and that person put him on a three-way call and called me for him? Wouldn't that let him skip the recording and everything else?"

"I'd have to check into that, but it might work," Cooper said. "It would be pretty stupid if that were the case. All those calls are recorded. If Peters or Wolff called you from prison, he'd be found out pretty quick."

"I suppose, but I should go with you if you're going to question Peters. He might say something that I can identify."

"I don't want you along if it's going to bother you," he said. "Besides, it's a long shot as it is."

"I'm sorry I haven't been doing better," Jayla said. "I'm stronger than that."

"I know you are," he said warmly.

"We both have to get past this, and the best way to do that is to find out the truth," she responded. "I want to help you."

"Good. I can use all the help I can get." He didn't tell her that he wanted to keep her close and not only to keep her safe.

They drove for a few minutes in silence.

"Is Mary Ann aware of the phone call?" he asked.

Jayla blinked. "Why do you ask?"

"I think she should know," Cooper said. "Did you tell her about the call?"

"I didn't want to scare her," she said.

"Scare her? She lives with you. She's in as much danger as you are. You don't think she should know?"

"I tried to get her to go stay with our parents for a few days," Jayla answered, "but she refused."

"Why?"

"She said she knew I was upset by everything that was happening and didn't want to leave me alone."

"Both of you should go," he suggested.

She shook her head. "They live too far away."

Cooper knew the drive from her parents' house to the station was at least two hours depending on traffic. It wouldn't be practical for the sisters to commute to work every day. Still, it would have made him feel better about the situation.

"Stanley promised to assign a couple of officers to watch the house," Jayla reminded him.

"Yeah, he did. I hope we'll get to the bottom of this before the officers are called somewhere else."

"Nobody's threatened me," she added. "Nobody's said anything obscene. I probably couldn't even make a case for harassment."

"You don't think he's trying to frighten and intimidate you?"

"I'll admit it's very creepy. But if it's the same person who killed Jill and Katie, then what would he want with me? I made it pretty clear in my statement that I didn't remember much about that call. I don't know anything about the case otherwise. I mean, besides what you've told me and what I've heard from Stanley and the other guys. What's the point?"

"I don't like you and Mary Ann being there by yourselves."

"We're always there by ourselves."

"No," he said grimly. "You sometimes work opposite shifts, so you're not always home at the same time."

"She's there by herself late at night when I'm on duty," Jayla conceded. "She's always been independent, so I've never worried about her. You don't think this guy would do something to her, do you?"

"It's hard to say." Cooper thought for a minute. "What if you came to stay at my place temporarily?"

She raised her eyebrows slightly. "I don't know about that."

"I mean both of you," he clarified. "You two could stay there and still be reasonably close to your jobs. I could stay at your place and keep an eye on everything. Then if the guy calls you, he would think you were still at home, but if he tried anything, I'd be there waiting for him."

"That's kind of you, but I don't think it's a good idea." Jayla smiled, obviously trying to play down her fear. "Besides, Lizzie would miss you too much."

Cooper grinned. "I'm sure she'd prefer sharing the house with you and Mary Ann."

"So what now?" Jayla asked.

"Do you have to work today?"

"Yes, but not until tonight. What do you have in mind?"

"I want to see if Brandon can help us track down Eric at one of the clubs," he replied. "He might know him or the band he manages."

"I'd like to hear what he has to say."

Cooper pulled over and called Brandon, then put the phone on speaker so they could both talk.

The phone rang twice before going to voice mail.

"Brandon, it's Cooper. Give me a call when you can. I need your help on a case. Thanks." He sighed when he hung up.

"He's probably busy," Jayla said. "He always was."

"He's got a lot going on," he said. "But I was hoping to get some kind of lead we could follow up on immediately."

"Maybe he'll call back soon," she said.

"There's no use sitting here and waiting for him." Cooper smiled. "I should check on Lizzie and see if she's still busy with her toys. The more bored she gets at my place, the more likely I am to find the toilet paper shredded."

Jayla laughed. "You'll have to let me meet her sometime."

He glanced at her out of the corner of his eye. "You could meet her now if you wanted to."

"Sure. Why not?"

Cooper was glad that Jayla had agreed because he didn't want to drop her off at home. She was becoming more important to him every second he was around her. He'd missed her something fierce.

But he also felt a twinge of anxiety. He knew he was falling for Jayla all over again. Would it end in heartache once more?

Jayla told herself that Cooper's invitation to meet Lizzie didn't mean anything. He was only being nice because she had gone to the pet store with him and helped pick out the toys. And because she was assisting him in this investigation. Not for any other reason. She would have been a fool to think otherwise.

Soon Cooper pulled up to a small ranch-style house with a two-car garage.

When they walked inside, he showed her around since she hadn't seen it before.

Jayla was impressed that the place was so neat and clean, but she wasn't surprised. Cooper had always been tidy. "It's very nice."

"Thanks," he said. "When I have some spare time, I want to finish some minor repairs and decorate a bit more."

She regarded the mostly bare walls. "That's a good idea. I think that will help it feel more like home for you."

"Since we didn't see Lizzie on our tour of the house, I'm guessing she's hiding under the bed." Cooper led the way to his bedroom, then got down on his hands and knees and peered under the bed. "Yep, there she is. Lizzie, come meet a new friend."

After a few moments of coaxing, he had to give up. "I'm sorry, but she won't come out."

"She's been through a lot," Jayla said. "I don't blame her for being skittish."

"Maybe next time," he said.

She averted her eyes, hoping she wasn't blushing. Did he really want her to come over again?

"Are you hungry?" Cooper asked. "I could make some turkey sandwiches."

She nodded and followed him into the kitchen.

He retrieved the sandwich fixings and a pitcher of iced tea from the fridge. "I'm anxious to hear from Brandon. I hope he calls soon."

"Me too," Jayla said.

"Do you want to do the tea?" Cooper asked as he prepared the sandwiches.

"Sure." She removed two glasses from the cupboard he indicated and poured the tea.

They set the plates, glasses, and napkins on the table, then sat down across from each other.

As Jayla took a sip of her iced tea, she wondered what to say. It felt strange but nice being in Cooper's kitchen.

Cooper talked a little more about the case as he ate his sandwich. Then he caught Jayla's eye. He put a finger to his lips and motioned toward the doorway.

She turned and saw an adorable tabby cat with green eyes.

Lizzie slowly stepped into the kitchen and sidled over to the table. She brushed past Cooper's legs, then approached Jayla. After rubbing her head against Jayla's legs, the cat sat down and gazed up at her expectantly.

Jayla smiled.

Lizzie hopped onto her lap, then curled up and purred.

Jayla lightly ran her hand down the cat's back. When she glanced at Cooper, he was grinning.

"Lizzie is smart," he said. "She can tell a good person a mile away."

"She's precious," Jayla murmured, stroking the cat's head.

As they finished their lunch in companionable silence, Jayla felt completely at peace. She was comforted by the sweet cat on her lap almost as much as by Cooper's presence.

Jayla stood and stretched, then checked the clock on the wall above her desk at the police station. It was nearly midnight.

She had enjoyed spending time with Cooper and Lizzie. Being in Cooper's house had felt natural—and the feeling disturbed her.

When Cooper had dropped Jayla off at home, he'd promised to tell her when he heard from Brandon. He hadn't mentioned when they would see each other again, and Jayla tried not to feel disappointed. Once again, she reminded herself that they were only working together on a case. Their relationship was over.

Jayla sat down when a new call popped up on the computer-aided dispatch system. While the 911 operator was still on the phone, the CAD sent pertinent information to dispatch so officers could respond as quickly as possible. Jayla immediately checked to see which units were currently available.

She frowned when she saw it was an attempted breaking and entering. There was a woman alone in the house.

Then the address came through. It was her own.

After Cooper had taken Jayla home, he'd stopped at the club where Brandon was playing. His friend hadn't returned his call, so Cooper had decided it was a good opportunity to listen to jazz and also talk to him face-to-face. Unfortunately, Brandon didn't know anyone named Eric or Evan who fit the description, but he'd promised to ask around and put Cooper in touch with anyone who could help.

On his way home, Cooper listened to his police scanner as usual. Suddenly, he heard a call for Jayla's address.

He jammed his foot on the accelerator and tried to calm down. Jayla was still at work. She was safe, but Mary Ann was home alone. Jayla would have heard the call too. If it hadn't come directly to her, he was sure that one of the other dispatchers would have mentioned it to her. Attempted breaking and entering. *Attempted*, he reminded himself. Not actual burglary. Not assault.

Not murder.

At this time of night, it was hard to find a place to park, especially with a squad car parked in front of Jayla's house, blocking part of the street as its lights flashed red and blue. Still, Cooper managed to claim a space about halfway down the block. It was a short jog to Jayla's front door.

He knocked and then pushed the door open. "Jayla? Mary Ann?"

The sisters were huddled together on the sofa, and Officer Kent was sitting in a chair across from them, taking notes.

Officer Daniels stood nearby, his arms crossed over his broad chest and displeasure evident on his features. "I should have known you'd show up."

"I heard the call come through." Cooper walked around to the back of the couch and put his arms around Jayla and Mary Ann. "Are you both okay?"

"Yeah," Mary Ann said. Tears welled in her eyes, and she blotted them away with the wad of tissues in her hand.

"You got here fast," Jayla said, sounding more angry than afraid.

"I went to hear Brandon play," he told her, "and I was on my way home."

"Did you ask him about Eric?"

He smiled slightly. "We have more important things to talk about. I'll tell you what he said in a little while."

"I think we have everything we need to start with," Kent said, getting to his feet. "We'll stay close the rest of the night. Call if you need us."

"What happened?" Cooper asked.

"It was reported as an attempted breaking and entering," Daniels said. "They can tell you more about it. We're going to cruise the neighborhood and see if we can track down anybody who fits the description."

"What little description we have," Kent added. He turned to the sisters. "Will you two be all right?"

"Yes," Jayla said, her voice low and tight. "Thanks, guys."

"We won't be far off," Daniels said. "Call us if you need to."

"We will," Jayla said.

"And lock this door," Daniels ordered.

"I'll do it," Cooper said, following the officers to the door and locking it after them. Then he sat down on the couch next to Jayla. "Tell me about it."

"I went to bed when Jayla left for work and then read for a while," Mary Ann said. "I guess I fell asleep with the light on, but the rest of the house was dark. I woke up when somebody started pounding on the front door. I didn't know who it would be so late, and I got my phone and went to see."

"I'm glad you took your phone," Cooper remarked.

"I was really quiet going to the door," Mary Ann continued. "I wanted to look through the peephole without letting him know I was there."

"And?" Cooper prompted.

"I couldn't tell much," Mary Ann answered. "I always leave the porch light on when Jayla's out at night, so I could see well enough. But the man wore a baseball cap pulled low, and his jacket collar covered the rest of his face."

"What kind of cap?" Cooper asked. "Rangers?"

"No, it was plain," Mary Ann said. "Black or navy, I think."

"And the jacket?"

"Black."

"Nobody wears a jacket when it's this warm," Jayla said scornfully. "Not unless he's trying to not be recognized."

"What else?" Cooper asked Mary Ann.

"When I saw him standing there, I knew he was a stranger," Mary Ann said. "I kept still, hoping he'd go away." Her voice shook. "Then he pounded on the door again and called Jayla's name."

Cooper winced. "Was he yelling or what?"

"No, it was loud enough for me to hear, but it was still pretty low," Mary Ann answered. "I was about to call 911 when he started rattling the door, trying to open it." She shivered.

"It's okay," Jayla soothed, hugging her sister closer. "Take your time."

Mary Ann took a deep breath. "Anyway, I didn't know what to do, so I told him the police were on the way and he'd better leave." She swallowed a sob. "Then he laughed. It was so awful that I almost couldn't breathe. It was exactly like Jayla said."

"Like Jayla said?" Cooper echoed. He glanced at Jayla, and she appeared queasy.

Mary Ann nodded. "Like what she heard in that 911 call."

"What happened after that?" he asked.

"He asked for Jayla. I told him she wasn't here, and I repeated that the police were coming." Mary Ann drew another deep breath and squeezed her eyes shut. "He said to tell Jayla that she'd better forget about what happened in apartment four. The more she remembers, the more dangerous it will be for her and everybody she loves."

Cooper's blood was boiling, but he managed to keep his voice even. "Did he say anything else?"

"No. He rattled the doorknob one more time and then took off."

"Which way?"

"I don't know," Mary Ann said. "I couldn't tell. It was too dark once he left the porch."

"What else did you notice about him?" Cooper asked. "Was he tall or short? What kind of build? Did you see his hair?"

"No, I couldn't see his hair because his collar was turned up. He had on black gloves." Mary Ann sniffled. "He was tall with an athletic build."

"Did you notice any other physical characteristics?"

Mary Ann shook her head. "He didn't want me to be able to recognize him."

"It's okay," Jayla told her sister. "It's all over now."

"How do you know he won't come back?" Mary Ann asked, suddenly pushing her away. "What if I'm alone again? Or you're alone?"

Jayla gave Cooper a helpless look.

He winced. If this was the same guy who killed Jill Kinner, he should have been off the street a year ago. And he would have been if Cooper had done his job correctly. "I'm sorry. It's true that we don't know who it is. But we're doing all we can to find the guy who killed Katie Myers and Jill Kinner."

Mary Ann got up and pushed her bangs off her forehead. "I can't stay here anymore."

"I'll be here." Jayla stood and put her arm around her sister. "You won't be alone anymore tonight."

"What about tomorrow?" Mary Ann demanded. "And after that? Are we both supposed to hide in here for the next few weeks or months until the police think they have the killer and then hope they're right?"

"Why don't you stay with Mom and Dad like we talked about?" Jayla asked. "It would be a longer drive, but it would be worth your peace of mind."

"What about you?" Mary Ann asked. "He was after *you*."

"I know," Jayla murmured.

Mary Ann stood there for a long moment. "I'm going to take some aspirin and try to go to sleep." She left the room.

"We'll be here," Cooper called after her.

Jayla gave him an apologetic smile. "Would you like a cup of coffee or something?"

"Coffee would be great, but I'm already plenty wound up. I don't need anything else to keep me awake."

"I know what you mean. I'll make decaf."

He followed her into the small galley kitchen. "Maybe you and Mary Ann should both go stay with your parents."

"I'm not sure about that." She prepped the coffee maker, then set two mugs on the counter.

"Hey," he said, picking up one of the mugs and admiring the green-and-white logo on the side. "My favorite."

"Go Stars," Jayla said as she retrieved the cream and sugar.

"I didn't know if you would have kept them." Cooper had given her a set of the mugs as a present. "That was after we went to our first hockey game together."

"When I didn't know offside from icing."

"You made up for it later," he teased. "I was just hoping you might enjoy the game or at least tolerate it. I had no idea I was creating a monster."

She grinned. "It's definitely the coolest game there is."

"All that ice," he joked.

"Probably." Jayla reached for his cup when the coffee maker beeped.

Cooper put his hand over hers. "I'm sorry this happened."

She took the cup. "I'm sorry too, but it's not my fault. And it's not yours."

"I should have been there for you," he admitted. "All this time."

"And this guy would still be doing what he's been doing anyway, wouldn't he?"

"Not if I had done my job in the first place," Cooper argued.

Jayla filled both cups with coffee. "He didn't come here because of your job. He came here because of mine. With that recording missing, I'm the only one who knows what he sounds like and what he said."

"At least he thinks you know."

She gave him a cup of coffee and put sugar in her own. When he was done with the cream, they went back to the sofa.

"I'm trying to remember," Jayla said, putting her cup on the coffee table in front of them. "This year's been hard."

"Yeah," he said almost under his breath.

"It hurt a lot when you left. I missed you. More than I thought I could miss anybody. I tried to understand what you were going through after Jill's murder and recovering from getting shot. I still don't quite understand why you think it was your fault that she was killed."

Cooper set his cup down and rubbed his eyes. "When I arrived at the scene, I stopped to find out what the situation was, who was involved, and anything else Mrs. Calvin could tell me. I should have immediately gone to the apartment and kicked that door down. Maybe I could have saved her."

"And maybe not." Jayla gently pulled his hand away from his face and peered deeply into his eyes. "What were you trained to do in those situations?"

"To learn as much as I could before going in."

"Why?"

"So I could handle it better."

"And save people's lives," she added.

"But I didn't. Jill died anyway."

"She might have already been dead when you arrived," she reasoned. "You said it was quiet by the time you got there. The coroner couldn't set the time of death to the exact minute it happened. You don't know."

He turned away from her and swallowed hard.

"What are you actually blaming yourself for?" she asked softly.

Cooper shook his head, avoiding her gaze.

Jayla slipped her hand into his. "Tell me."

"I was nervous going in," he began, "but I always was anyway. You can't predict what's going to happen in those kinds of situations."

"That's natural," she murmured. "And you went in anyway. Courage isn't the absence of fear, remember? It's pushing through the fear to do what needs to be done."

"The truth is, I was terrified," Cooper admitted, his voice suddenly hoarse. "When I was lying there with a bullet in my head. When I didn't know if I was going to make it." He licked his dry lips. "I didn't want to die."

Jayla squeezed his hand and remained silent.

"I guess it made me think," he said. "Jill Kinner died. I could have died. There was nothing I could do about it. Maybe next time it would be you. Or Kelly or anybody else close to me. I didn't want to deal with it. I couldn't deal with it. So I ran."

"I wish you had run to me instead of away from me." She wiped the tears in her eyes.

Cooper had to fight the tears that burned in his own. "Me too," he whispered.

"I've missed you so much all this time," Jayla said. "I thought if I gave you enough time—"

He put his arms around her and pulled her close. "I'm so sorry," he said against her soft hair. "I didn't mean to hurt you. I only wanted you to be safe. I couldn't stand it if anything happened to you."

She didn't say a word. Instead, she slipped her arms around him, holding him tight.

"I haven't been the same without you," Cooper said. "Can you ever forgive me?"

Jayla nodded against his shoulder, then nestled against him, not moving.

After a little while, he felt her shaking. "Are you okay?" He lifted her tearstained face and realized she was laughing. He couldn't help but laugh too.

Jayla kissed his cheek. "I feel better now."

"I'm glad. I've missed you so much." Cooper hugged her tightly once again. More than anything, he wanted to kiss her in the sweet way he used to before everything had fallen apart last year, but he didn't. Things had been crazy in the past few days, and he knew the emotional roller coaster she'd been on. He'd been in the seat right next to her.

Still, he couldn't stop smiling. They hadn't worked everything out. It wasn't what it had been, but maybe it could eventually be better than ever. If he had learned nothing else in the past year, he had learned there wasn't anyone he wanted more than Jayla.

"You never did tell me what Brandon said about Eric," Jayla commented, a hopeful light in her eyes.

"I'm sorry to say it didn't end up being anything," Cooper said. "Brandon knows a few Evans and Erics, but none of them fit the description we have."

The light in her eyes dimmed.

"But he told me that he'd ask around," Cooper said. "He's met a lot of guys in the music business. He promised to stay in touch."

"Yeah, that's good," she whispered, clearly disappointed.

He gently lifted her chin so she had to meet his eyes. "We're going to get the guy who killed Jill and Katie and the one who was here tonight. Maybe there are three different men. Maybe there's one. But we're going to figure it out, and we're going to catch them. I'll do everything I can to make sure you and Mary Ann are safe."

"I know," Jayla said, and she touched her lips lightly to his. "Thank you."

Feeling more than a touch of regret, he pulled away from her. "Are you and Mary Ann going to be okay here tonight?"

She nodded. "We'll be fine. Kent and Daniels will stay close. Whoever that was, he knows his message got through. There's no reason for him to come back."

Cooper finished his coffee, then stood up. "You'll want to get some sleep, and I'd better do the same. I need to be fresh if I'm going to find the guy who was here tonight."

Jayla walked with him to the door and kissed his cheek. "Call me."

He gave her a wink. "You bet."

She smiled and closed the door.

Cooper stood outside, waiting until he heard the lock, the dead bolt, and the chain set in place. Then he walked to his car, got in, and started the engine.

He prowled the neighborhood for a few minutes, searching for anyone who might fit Mary Ann's description of the man who had terrorized her earlier. But the street was quiet, except for the two times he passed Kent and Daniels driving around too.

The third time, Daniels rolled his eyes from the passenger seat and mouthed, "Go home."

Cooper gave him a wave of surrender and obeyed.

Jayla's shift was scheduled to start at noon the next day. After what had happened, she hadn't thought she would be able to sleep that night. But once she had checked on Mary Ann and found her sound asleep, she realized how exhausted she was and went to bed. Jayla slept heavily until she had to get up for work.

She felt a little groggy as she drove to the police station, but she couldn't help smiling when she thought about Cooper. Before Jill Kinner's murder last year, she had thought they could work out anything together. Now she was beginning to think so again.

Jayla greeted a few officers as she walked into the building and headed to her workstation. She was surprised to see a blank envelope waiting for her when she got to her desk, and she sat down to open it. Jayla pulled out a sheet of copier paper. Glued to the page was one word that had been cut out from a newspaper headline.

*Forget.*

Jayla gasped and dropped the piece of paper. As she stared at the note, she attempted to slow her breathing and calm down.

*Forget.*

That was all it said, but it was enough. It was the same message the awful man last night had told Mary Ann to give her. He wanted her to forget what she'd heard, what she couldn't really remember anyway except for the man's terrifying voice. A voice Mary Ann had described the same way.

*Forget.*

Jayla rushed into the corridor, wondering who could help her. Stanley would be the best option. He was already involved in the case. Walking faster, she peeked into the interrogation rooms and a couple of meeting rooms. There was no sign of him anywhere. Then she backtracked and rushed to the reception desk. Sheila knew where everybody was most of the time.

Sheila sat at her desk with a candy bar and a diet drink. "I figure the one offsets the other," she said with a self-conscious giggle, then turned serious. "What's wrong? You're white as a sheet."

"I'm fine," Jayla said. "Have you seen Stanley lately?"

"He walked by a little while ago," Sheila replied. "You didn't see him? He was headed your way, but that could have been right before you came in. He was carrying his usual stack of papers and folders."

"Did he have an envelope?" Jayla asked. "One of the long ones?"

Sheila shrugged. "Maybe. I didn't particularly notice."

"Did he mention where he was going?"

"Yes, he was heading to the captain's office."

Jayla frowned. Her workstation wasn't on the way from here to the captain's office. "Thanks." She practically ran to the captain's office, but Stanley wasn't there.

As she turned to go, Stanley suddenly appeared behind her, and she practically jumped out of her skin. Where else had he been?

"What's up?" Stanley asked.

Jayla noticed he was carrying his usual paperwork like Sheila said, but she didn't see any envelopes. "I was just wondering if you had any news on the Myers case." She didn't want to say anything to him about the note that had been left for her. Not yet.

"Not really," Stanley said. "Daniels told me what happened at your place last night. I read the report too. I'm sorry. Is your sister okay?"

"She's pretty scared, but she's fine."

"I told Daniels to keep a close watch on your place whenever he's on duty," Stanley said. "Same for the other units that patrol your area."

"Thank you," Jayla said. She needed to sit down and collect her thoughts. "Well, I'd better get to work. They're going to be asking where I am."

Stanley nodded. "Take care."

Jayla walked toward her desk, feeling his eyes on her until she rounded the corner and was out of his sight. Stanley was acting strangely. She almost gasped when an idea occurred to her.

Was he somehow involved?

When she got back to her workstation, the note and the envelope were gone.

"Why didn't you take the note and the envelope with you?" Cooper asked Jayla when she called to tell him what had happened.

"I didn't want to touch it any more than I already had in case we could get fingerprints from it," she replied. "How could I have been so foolish?"

"No, what you did makes perfect sense," he assured her. "But I wish that you had called somebody to come see it instead of going to get someone."

"Me too," Jayla said miserably.

"I doubt there would be any prints on it besides yours anyway," Cooper said, his voice low and soothing. "And the note contained one word?"

"Yes. 'Forget.'"

"Nothing about the paper or envelope that would give any clues?"

"No, it was plain paper like you put in your copier or printer," she answered. "It came in a business-size white envelope."

"Was it one of those security envelopes?" he asked. "The kind that have printing inside so nobody can read the contents without opening it?"

"No, it was plain." Jayla sighed. "Everything was plain."

"What about the newsprint? Anything notable about the font the word was printed in?"

"Not really," she said. "The letters were large, like they were from a headline."

Cooper was quiet for a bit. "Did the newsprint appear recent? Was it yellowed at all?"

"I don't think so, but I only saw it for a few seconds," Jayla said. "It startled me at first, and I dropped it so I wouldn't get my prints on it any more than I already had."

"Then what did you do?"

"I went searching for—" She stopped before admitting her suspicions about Stanley.

Cooper and Stanley were good friends. Stanley had shown Cooper the ropes when he was a rookie. They'd even been assigned to the same patrol unit for a few months. Cooper liked and respected Stanley.

"What is it?"

"I need to talk to you about something," Jayla said, keeping her voice low. "But I can't do it at the moment. I've got to go on duty. I'm scheduled for a break at three. Can I call you then?"

"Of course, but you'd better not forget," he said. "I'll be at the station searching for you if you don't call me right on time."

She smiled, even though he couldn't see it. "I'll call you. Don't worry."

"I'm glad we talked yesterday," Cooper admitted.

"Me too," Jayla said, feeling her heart soar. "It's been too long."

"It has. I'll talk to you later." He hung up.

She was glad that he hadn't told her again that it had been his fault. The circumstances were hard, and she definitely understood his fears. She also understood how hard it must have been for a guy like him to admit he had been afraid at all.

*Please, God, look out for him*, she prayed. *And help us figure out what's going on.*

It was a busy afternoon as usual. When her break came at three o'clock, Jayla grabbed her purse and hurried out to her car. She turned on the engine so she could stay cool and called Cooper.

He picked up on the first ring. "Good thing you called. I was about to come get you."

She forced a laugh. Though the time had come, she hesitated to broach the subject of Stanley. But she still couldn't shake the sinking feeling that the officer was somehow involved.

"Now tell me what's going on," Cooper said.

"Something's bothering me."

"And that is?"

"I don't know who could have left that envelope for me unless it was someone inside the station," Jayla said.

"Do you suspect someone in particular?"

"I do. After I discovered the note, I talked to Sheila. She told me that she had seen someone going toward my workstation with a stack of folders and papers. She said he was going to see the captain, but the captain's office isn't in that direction. Nobody would need to pass my area to go see the captain."

"That's true," he said. "So who was it?"

"You're not going to like this."

"We need the truth whether any of us likes it or not."

She took a deep breath. "It was Stanley."

Cooper didn't reply.

"Are you still there?" she asked after several seconds passed.

"Yeah," he said on a heavy breath. "I didn't want to bring it up, but I was already wondering. Since that 911 recording was taken from evidence, I've been trying to figure out who could have had access to it. It must have been someone at the station. A cop."

Jayla cringed when she detected the hurt in his voice. "I can't be sure about Stanley," she said, hoping her suspicions were wrong. "Maybe he was on his way somewhere else before he went to see the captain."

"Maybe so."

"Or it could have been somebody else who works at the station," she suggested. "In maintenance or another department."

"They wouldn't have access to evidence rooms or case files," Cooper pointed out.

Her heart thudded in her chest. "Case files?"

"I'm still wondering about those statements Wolff and his wife made about the Kinner murder. I've read them before. Not recently, but not so long ago that it doesn't make me wonder. Stanley says he doesn't remember them actually saying her boyfriend could have been the killer. I don't remember it either, but it's there now."

"What are you saying?" Jayla asked, her mind spinning. "That those records could have been altered?"

"Yes, they could have been," he replied. "If somebody is determined and rich enough, they could bribe anyone. Would it be any harder to bribe a clerk than a cop?" He took a deep breath. "Even a cop as good as Stanley."

"There are also the copies Wolff's lawyers would have," she said, "but I guess they would be the easiest ones to replace."

"Money buys a lot of cooperation."

"I can't say for sure that Stanley was doing anything he shouldn't have been," Jayla said.

"What makes you suspicious of him?"

"I don't know exactly what it was. But it seemed strange when Sheila said he'd been heading that way right before I came in. And then he showed up behind me when I was searching for him."

"As if he'd been by your desk again," Cooper said, finishing her thought.

"Exactly. And the note and envelope had disappeared when I went back to my desk." She sighed. "I don't want to stir up anything in case we're wrong."

"I totally agree," Cooper said firmly. "But I'll do it if it's necessary, and I don't want you to feel bad about mentioning it to me."

"Thanks," Jayla said, relieved.

"Did you ask around your area to see if anybody had been there? Anybody at your workstation particularly? Anybody who didn't usually have business there?"

"I asked around after I talked to you," she answered. "Nobody saw anything unusual."

"Well, watch for anything out of the ordinary," he advised. "It wouldn't hurt to ask around again. Sometimes people think of things after you've questioned them."

"I'll do that."

"You didn't happen to see Kelly around there lately, did you?"

"No. Is he on duty?"

"I don't know," Cooper said. "I'll give him a call and tell him what you said—"

"Please don't tell him about my suspicions," Jayla interrupted.

"Don't worry. He'll keep quiet about it. All I want him to do is keep an eye on Stanley for me. He can do it without making a big deal of it. That won't hurt anything, will it?"

"Not at all."

"Good." He paused. "When are you done for the day?"

"Eight."

"Want to have dinner?"

"Sure," she said, hoping she didn't sound too excited. "What do you have in mind?"

"I'll come get you at eight. Sound good?"

"That would be great." Jayla checked the clock in her dashboard. "I have to get back to work. I only wanted to tell you what's going on here."

"Thanks. I'm glad you did. And be careful. I don't like the idea of somebody at the station being behind this. I don't like leaving you vulnerable."

"I'll stay on guard."

"Make sure you do," Cooper said. "See you at eight." He hung up.

She slipped her phone into her purse, turned off the engine, and hurried back into the station.

Stanley was walking out. "Where have you been? I thought you were on duty."

Jayla forced a smile. "I am, but I had something to do on my break."

"You and your sister be careful, okay? And let me know if you have any more incidents like last night."

"Thanks." She stood at the door and watched him get into his unmarked car and drive away.

She shivered as she thought about her conversation with Cooper. Was Stanley someone they could trust?

After Cooper hung up with Jayla, he called his brother.

The call went straight to Kelly's voice mail, and Cooper left a message. "I don't know what your schedule is, but I need to talk to you. It's about the Myers case, and it's important. Keep it between you and me for now. Call me."

As soon as Cooper disconnected, Brandon texted him about a couple of guys who might be able to identify the mysterious Eric. Brandon invited Cooper to meet him and his bandmates at the club where they would be playing that night.

Cooper filled Lizzie's food bowl and freshened her water. The cat twined around his legs. She was getting friendlier all the time. Or maybe she was just hungry. Cooper smiled when he remembered how taken Lizzie had been with Jayla. He hoped Jayla would visit again soon.

"I'll be home later," Cooper told the cat. "Be good. No shredding the toilet paper."

Lizzie jumped onto the sofa and curled up, watching him as he left.

Cooper drove to the club and found a parking spot near the front door. When he walked inside, he spotted Brandon sitting at one of the tables with two other men.

Brandon smiled and motioned Cooper over.

Cooper approached the table. "Thanks for getting in touch."

"No problem," Brandon said. His dark hair was slicked back, and his goatee was neatly trimmed as always. He wore a black suit with a pink shirt and a paisley silk tie.

"You're getting bland in your old age," Cooper teased.

"You have to keep up," Brandon replied.

Cooper laughed. "I could never keep up with you."

"Have a seat," Brandon said.

Cooper sat down next to him.

Brandon gestured to the tall man on the other side of the table. "I think you already know Johnny."

"Yes, it's good to see you again," Cooper said. He had met Johnny a couple of times, and he admired the man's ease with both English and Spanish. In a city like Dallas, it would be useful for a private investigator to speak Spanish, especially if he looked like he didn't.

Johnny nodded a greeting. He was elegantly dressed, with brown skin and shiny, slicked-down black hair.

"And this is Marty," Brandon said.

Marty was a stranger to Cooper. He was lean and sunburned, and he wore the most expensive gold watch Cooper had ever seen. Various tattoos peeked out of his sleeves, and there was a large tattoo on his neck.

Cooper didn't miss the fact that neither of them offered their last names. He nodded at Marty, then addressed Brandon. "Did you tell the guys what I'm after?"

"You want to know about somebody named Eric or Evan who manages a band, right?" Johnny asked. "There are a lot of guys with those names."

"How many of them have long, dark hair and extensive tattoos on their arms?" Cooper asked.

"Like sleeves?" Marty asked.

"Possibly," Cooper said. "I don't know the details, but I heard it was a lot."

Marty and Johnny glanced at each other and shrugged.

Johnny lit a cigarette and narrowed his eyes. "What do you want with this guy?"

"I'm hoping to get some information about a woman who was murdered last year," Cooper replied.

"That's a long time ago," Marty said. "Why the renewed interest?"

"Because another woman was killed last week," Cooper said. "Both of them were in their own apartment. Alone. I don't know if this guy had anything to do with it or not, but I don't want somebody else getting murdered."

Johnny frowned. "My little sister was killed three years ago by some dealers who were after her boyfriend."

"I remember," Brandon said grimly.

Marty nodded. "We'll help you if we can."

"Thanks," Cooper said. "So what have you got?"

"I know two guys named Evan," Johnny said. "One has tattoos all over, but he's pretty short and skinny. The other one's a big guy. He has long, dark hair, but he doesn't have any tattoos. I don't know anyone named Eric in the business."

"I know four Evans," Marty offered. "Two manage bands, but they don't fit the description at all. The third is my next-door neighbor, and he's about eighty."

"And the fourth one?" Cooper asked.

"My dad," Marty said with a sly grin. "And he despises tattoos."

Cooper chuckled. "What about Eric?"

"I know a couple, but they're not in the business," Marty said. "Well, there was one before that. He managed a punk band years ago, but he went out to LA. I haven't seen him since. Sorry. I guess we're coming up empty for you."

"His name wasn't Eric, but I saw a guy a few days ago at another club," Johnny said. "He fit your description."

Cooper leaned forward in his chair. "What was his name?"

"You remember him, don't you?" Johnny asked Marty.

"Yeah," Marty said. "Big guy, long hair, sleeves. He had some pretty wild ink too. I meant to ask him where he got it."

"Do you recall his name?" Cooper pressed.

"Tony?" Johnny said. "I don't really remember. But if we see him again, we can give you a call."

"That would be great." Cooper gave business cards to the two men. "You know how important this is, don't you? Even on a cold case."

Johnny tucked the card into his silver cigarette case. "They never found the men who killed my sister. I know it's important."

Cooper thought for a moment, and then he took out another business card and wrote on the back of it. "When I get this case solved, I'm going to rattle a few cages for your sister, okay? For now, I'm going to mention her case to this friend of mine. He's the one who works on cold cases for the DPD. He might be able to get somebody to check into it again."

"I'd appreciate that," Johnny said, taking the card and putting it with the other one. "Thank you."

"Thanks for talking to me." Cooper shook Johnny's hand, then Marty's. "You two call me if you come across that guy again."

Marty nodded. "If he killed those women, we don't need him around here."

"Tell Jessica I said hello," Cooper said, shaking his old friend's hand last of all.

"She wanted to come with me to see you," Brandon responded. "She said to tell you not to be a stranger."

"No stranger than usual," Cooper told him with a grin. "Thanks again, guys."

Once he was back in his car, he sat there and considered the murder cases. His thoughts returned to the apartment house, and he wondered who had bought it from the elderly landlady. He called Mrs. Calvin.

"What can I do for you?" she asked. "I'm getting ready to close on my building, and then I'm going directly to Florida. I don't suppose I'll hear from you after this."

"That'll be a shame," Cooper said. "I'll have to start buying my own coffee."

Mrs. Calvin chuckled. "I guess you can manage it."

"I was curious about you selling that house," he said. "Did you have it on the market long?"

"I didn't have it on the market at all," she said.

"Really?" Cooper asked, trying to hide his surprise. "What happened?"

"I'd been thinking about selling it ever since what happened last year," Mrs. Calvin explained. "And my granddaughter's been after me to retire and move closer to her and her family. When somebody made me a good offer, I snatched it."

"I see. I don't want to pry into your business, so just tell me no if you don't want to answer."

"Oh, I will."

Cooper couldn't help but smile. "Was it an individual who made you the offer? Or a corporation?"

"It was one of those investment corporations," she replied. "Hold on. Let me grab the documents from the closing."

He heard the rustle of papers.

"It's a place called LL & Z Investment Properties," Mrs. Calvin said. "I never heard of them. But their earnest money was good, and their bank is ready to wire me the rest of the money once we finish signing all the papers."

Cooper had never heard of them either, and he made a note to check them out. "Do you have something with their address and the name of the person who's signing for them? Maybe a phone number?"

She shuffled a few more papers. "Alison Travers is the managing partner." Then she gave him an address in Dallas and a phone number.

He jotted down the information. "Thank you."

"Wait a minute," Mrs. Calvin said. "Am I getting ripped off or something?"

"No, don't worry. Your title company will make sure you get your money if you transfer the title. The company could be new to the area, so that might be the reason why you haven't heard of them. It doesn't mean they're doing anything illegal. You said their funds were good, right?"

"What they paid me so far, yes."

"The title company wouldn't do the deal if everything wasn't in line," Cooper assured her. "Who are you going through?"

She gave him the name of a well-known and highly respected title company that had been in the Dallas area for a long time.

"I think you're fine with them," he told her. "I didn't ask you about your buyer to get you rattled. I was merely curious about why they picked your building."

Mrs. Calvin huffed. "They know a prime property when they see one."

"I'm sure that's it," he said, smiling again.

"Have you found that man?" she demanded suddenly. "I don't want to hear about another murder next May."

"I'm working on it. And I'll call you when I catch him. How's that?"

"That's fine," Mrs. Calvin said. "Meanwhile, don't you let anybody be shooting you anymore, understand?"

"No, I don't plan to let that happen ever again."

"Good. Are you seeing that young lady you brought to my hotel?"

Cooper had to stifle a surprised laugh. "Uh, yeah, I suppose so."

"Well, you look out for her too," she advised. "I don't want to hear anything happened to her either."

"I definitely will," he promised. "Thanks for the information. Is somebody going with you to your closing?"

Mrs. Calvin huffed again. "My granddaughter. She thinks because I'm of a certain age, I don't know my own business."

"I'd never make the mistake of thinking that."

"You're a smart man," she said. "You find that murderer, you hear?"

"I will. Thank you. Be sure to send me your new address so I can mail you the coffee I promised you."

Mrs. Calvin laughed. "I'll do that."

As soon as Cooper hung up, he called the number she had given him. He got a recording that said he had reached LL & Z Investment Properties, assured him that his business was important to them, and asked him to leave a message. He disconnected without leaving a message, then glanced at the clock in his dashboard and saw that it was after business hours. He drove over to their office anyway.

The office was in a respectable part of town. They were closed, but the door had the company's name on it. He cupped his hands on either side of his face to block the sunlight so he could peer through the glass. The reception area was nice, and everything appeared new and stylish. It seemed to be a new investment company, nothing more. They popped up all the time in a busy city like Dallas.

He decided to research when the company had been incorporated and peruse the paperwork they had filed with the city, then returned to his car and headed home. About halfway there, his brother called him back.

"Got your message," Kelly said. "But I was still on duty, and you said you wanted to keep this between you and me. What's up?"

Cooper told him about the threatening note Jayla had received at the station. Then he described her suspicions about Stanley.

"No way," Kelly said. "Come on. Stanley?"

"She wasn't accusing him," Cooper clarified. "She was only wondering. Even if it isn't him, don't you think there has to be somebody at the station who's involved?"

"I don't know."

"Besides the note, there's the missing 911 recording, and I'm starting to think some of the evidence has been altered." Cooper told Kelly about the statements Wolff and his wife had made after the Kinner murder.

"Who would want to change the statements?" Kelly asked.

"Somebody who wants to have another suspect to blame."

"You mean if Wolff couldn't have murdered Katie Myers because he was in jail at the time and Peters has an alibi for it too."

"Maybe."

"Okay, it's possible he has an alibi," Kelly conceded. "If he does, then whoever is really behind it has to point the finger at someone else."

"Stanley investigated both murders, didn't he?"

"Yeah. So?"

"So nothing," Cooper said, exhaling heavily. "I don't know what I'm thinking except that you're around him a lot more than I am. Help me out by keeping your eyes open. See if he does anything weird."

"We're not reporting him, okay?"

"No. Not unless there's something to go on. I'm not ruining a guy's career over something I don't have any evidence for."

"Anybody at the station could have gotten to that recording and those statements," Kelly said. "And anybody could have left that note for Jayla. How is she doing?"

"I think she's okay. She gets off work at eight, and I'm going to take her to dinner."

"I see."

Cooper scowled. "What's that supposed to mean?"

"Nothing," Kelly said, but there was definitely a smirk in his voice.

"Don't be making a big deal over nothing," Cooper said. "I'd better not hear that Jen called Jayla to find out if we're back together."

"I'll keep it to myself." Kelly paused. "But are you?"

"Who wants to know?"

"Come on. It's me. Your favorite brother."

Cooper rolled his eyes. "You mean my only brother."

"Doesn't that make me all the more valuable?"

"It means you're priceless," Cooper said.

"As in, not worth anything," they both said at the same time.

It was an old joke between them, but it still made them laugh.

"I'm not sure about Jayla yet," Cooper admitted, serious again. "I love her. Don't tell anybody that, not even Jen. But she probably wouldn't consider seeing me again after—"

"You were a total idiot for most of a year?" Kelly interrupted.

"Yeah."

"She should have ripped you up one side and down the other."

"But that's not her," Cooper said. "It's never been her. I should have known all along that she'd understand."

"I guess she did," Kelly said. "All of us did. Everybody but you."

"I suppose I had to figure things out for myself," Cooper said. "But I'm sorry it took something like this to get me back in touch with Jayla."

"Sometimes there's absolutely no way around stubborn. Have you told Jayla that you still love her?" Kelly asked. "No, don't answer that. I know you. You'll shuffle around not saying anything for months until she has to ask you how you feel about her."

"I'll tell her," Cooper said, feeling a little annoyed because deep inside he knew his brother had hit the nail on the head.

"Don't wait too long," Kelly warned. "Otherwise, she might not be there by the time you get around to telling her."

"Thanks for cheering me up."

"I'm trying to help," Kelly explained. "I don't want you to lose her again."

"I don't either," Cooper said. "Don't mention what I told you about Stanley and Jayla, okay?"

"I won't, but I'll be watching."

"Thanks," Cooper said. "Are we still supposed to come over tomorrow at seven?"

"Definitely. We'll see you then."

"See you." Cooper smiled when he ended the call. He'd said that he loved Jayla, and he meant it.

Thank God she seemed willing to give him a second chance. He wasn't going to blow it this time.

As planned, Cooper picked Jayla up from the station at eight that evening. He took her to an Italian restaurant they had liked when they had dated. He'd thought it would be a nice place to start over again, and he was right.

Once he had made sure that Jayla and Mary Ann were doing well and that Jayla hadn't gotten any more threatening notes at work, the conversation moved to what they had each been doing in the past few months. In spite of all the time they'd spent together over the past week, they hadn't had a chance to catch up.

After an hour, their plates of chicken cannelloni and broccoli romano were only half eaten and the Italian cream cake was barely touched, but they still had a lot to talk about.

"Maybe we'd better get out of here," Cooper suggested. "They've got people waiting for our table, and the waiter has been glaring at us for the last ten minutes."

Jayla laughed softly. "He has not."

"Well, it's obvious that he wants to." He smiled. "What do you say? Would you like to come visit Lizzie for a few minutes?"

"Yes, I'd love to."

"Ever since she warmed up to you, she's been much braver," Cooper said. "And I found most of her toys in the bathtub this morning, so I know she's been enjoying them."

"That's great to hear," she said. "Lizzie's such a sweetheart."

"By the way, I called Katie Myers's dad."

"Her dad?"

Cooper nodded. "I told him I've been taking care of Lizzie. He said he'd come pick her up, but then he'd have to take her to a shelter. Katie's mom is allergic, so they can't have a cat."

"Oh no. Poor Lizzie."

"Don't worry. She's not going to a shelter." Cooper grinned. "I offered to keep her because I've grown pretty attached to her, and he said that was fine by him."

Jayla smiled. "I'm so glad. She's been through enough already without being uprooted again."

"Come on," he said. "Let's go see her."

She grabbed her purse from the back of the chair. "I'm ready."

Cooper paid the check, leaving a generous tip, and escorted Jayla back to his car.

"I meant to tell you that I got in touch with the TV station about those police shows Ray Jensen was talking about," he said. "A man took my e-mail address and agreed to let me know which episodes ran on the night of May 7, what time they aired, and where they were filmed."

"That's great," she said as she buckled her seat belt.

"I hope it is," Cooper said. "The man told me it might take a day or two."

"Maybe it'll help."

He shrugged and put the car into gear. "He wasn't very enthusiastic about the project. I'll give him a couple of days and then get in touch with his boss."

They had barely gotten out of the parking lot when his phone rang. Laurel Wolff's name and number came up on the display.

Jayla glanced at the screen and raised her eyebrows.

"Good evening," Cooper said as he answered. He put the call

on speakerphone. "What can I do for you?"

"I was wondering if you had any news for me yet," Laurel said. "Did you find out anything about Jill Kinner's boyfriend?"

"Nothing but dead ends so far," he answered. "Did your husband remember anything else about the guy?"

Laurel sighed. "No, Dane said she wouldn't say much about the man. But Dane told me how she tore into him for erasing the pictures on her phone. The other man appeared in a lot of the photos. Dane said that made it easier for him to end things with her."

"Anything else?"

"Dane wrote down the phone number she had in her call list," Laurel said. "Dane is pretty sure the man's name was Eric, and he believes the number must have been his."

"Does your husband still have the number?" Cooper asked.

"Dane doesn't know what happened to the slip of paper he wrote the number on," Laurel replied. "He said it was the back of a receipt from a restaurant."

"I guess that's long gone," Cooper said on a heavy breath.

"Hear me out. Ever since I talked to him, I've been trying to figure out where that receipt could be. I searched everywhere. Before all this happened, Dane played golf every chance he got in the spring. I finally went through his golf bag."

"Where was that?"

"It's been in the trunk of his car for more than a year," Laurel replied. "I hadn't even thought about it until I talked to him. He had a windbreaker stuffed in one of the pockets, and I remember the night that woman was killed was windy and rainy. I thought he could have had that windbreaker on when he broke up with her."

Cooper considered what she'd told him. It was possible. "Okay," he said, trying not to get his hopes up. "And?"

"I found a receipt for lunch at the club," Laurel said, almost breathless. "Our club, where he always played golf. On the back there was a phone number."

Cooper glanced at Jayla, his own breath coming a little faster. "Did you call the number?"

"Yes, and it rang and rang," Laurel said. "I thought you could trace it and discover who it belongs to."

"I can do that. Give me the number." He nodded toward the pen and notepad in the console between the seats.

Jayla grabbed them. As Laurel recited the number, Jayla jotted it down. It was a local area code.

Cooper might be able to connect it to an address, and he hoped it would be one here in town. "Let me see what I can dig up about this. I'll call you back when I know something."

"Do you think you'll learn something right away?" Laurel asked. "I'd very much like to hear something soon."

"I'll get on it now. If I uncover something and it's not too late, I'll call you."

"Please call me anytime," Laurel said. "I won't be able to rest until I hear from you." She took a shaky breath. "Or maybe I should take something to help me sleep until morning. I don't know. You can call anytime. I'll be here."

"I'll get back to you." As soon as Cooper ended the call, he called the number she had given him.

It rang and rang.

"She didn't get an answer either," Jayla said. "It might not be a valid number anymore."

"Then we'd get a message that it was no longer in use. This guy might only call out with that number."

"Don't remind me."

"Could that be the number from the call you got in the middle of the night?"

"I don't know. Let me check." She scanned her call list. "No, it's different."

They drove on for another few minutes. Still the phone rang. Still no answer.

"Might as well hang up," Jayla said.

"Let it ring."

They were almost to Cooper's house when the ringing stopped with a sudden click.

"What do you want?" The voice was low and dark, somewhere between a hiss and a growl.

Jayla gasped.

"Who is this?" Cooper asked, his voice hard. "Is this Eric?"

Jayla's heart raced. She knew the disturbing voice was the one from the phone call. Could it be the one from the 911 call too?

The man laughed. "I see your name. Cooper Cole."

Jayla wrapped her arms around herself and squeezed her eyes shut. She couldn't believe this was happening.

"Officer Cole," the man said. "Yes, I remember you. I heard you pulled through."

"Where are you?" Cooper demanded. "What do you want?"

"I want you to tell Jayla that I'll kill her," the man said. "I'll kill her and her sister if she doesn't shut up. Just like I killed that other woman in the apartment. She shouldn't have been there. That was Jill's place. Nobody can live there. I killed Jill there, and that makes it a shrine. Her shrine and mine."

Jayla bit her lip, trying to keep from screaming at him to shut up. To shut up and go away and never come back.

"You killed Jill Kinner?" Cooper asked. "Why?"

"So *he* couldn't have her," the man growled. "He'll go down for it, and I'll have her all to myself forever."

"Where are you?" Cooper repeated. "The police are going to catch you."

"Not in my shrine," the man said. "They're trying to tear it to pieces inside, but they can't. I won't let them."

Cooper pulled up to the corner and wheeled the car around the way they had come.

Jayla knew exactly where he was heading. The man was in apartment four as they spoke.

"What are you going to do?" Cooper asked evenly. Then he mouthed to Jayla, "Call the police. Quietly."

Jayla gripped her phone, feeling steadier with something specific to do. She dialed 911.

While the man ranted about Jill and his shrine, Jayla whispered into her phone, giving the 911 operator the situation and the address to the apartment house. "He's there now," she breathed. "Hurry." She ended the call.

"If they move somebody in this apartment again, I'll kill her too," the man said. "Every year on May 7. You couldn't stop me, Officer Cole." He laughed. "Oh, but you're not even an officer anymore, are you? I scared you. Next time I'll kill you. You know I will. You can feel it. You can never face me again."

Cooper's expression was like granite. Hard. Unreadable. Still, he was heading toward the apartment house. He wasn't turning back.

They were only a block away when Jayla heard the wail of sirens.

"You can't stop me," the man said. "I'll kill you for calling the cops."

She heard the echo of heavy steps on the other end of the line.

"Give yourself up," Cooper said. "You won't get away again."

"You'll never find me," the man said. "But I'll find you. Count on it."

The line went dead.

As they drove, Jayla texted Mary Ann that there were developments in the case and she'd likely be late coming home.

When they arrived at the apartment house, the lights were on upstairs and down. Whether that was because the remodelers didn't want people to think the place was abandoned or because Eric had flipped them on, Jayla wasn't sure. There was a police car in front with its lights flashing. Two officers exited the car. Jayla didn't know the younger man. The other one was Stanley.

Cooper put one finger to his lips, and they got out of his car.

"What's going on?" Stanley snapped.

"He's in there," Cooper said.

"Armed?"

"I can't say for sure, but I would guess so," Cooper answered. "He didn't mention a weapon, but he didn't sound like he'll just give himself up either."

Stanley crossed his arms over his chest. "What are you two doing here anyway?"

"Laurel found a phone number in her husband's belongings," Cooper explained. "She believes it's the number for Jill Kinner's boyfriend. It seems like we hit the jackpot."

"What else?" Stanley asked.

"He confessed to murdering both Jill and Katie," Cooper said. "He threatened to kill Jayla and her sister if Jayla identified him from the recording. He also threatened to kill me." He shrugged. "The usual stuff."

Stanley nodded. "He's in apartment four?"

"As far as I can tell," Cooper replied.

"The apartment overlooks the right side of the house," Stanley said. "That tree will keep him from shooting out the front window." He nudged the younger officer with him, the red and blue lights flashing over both of them. "Parker, tell Daniels and Kent that we think the suspect is armed and to stay away from the windows back there. Tell them to make sure nobody gets out the back."

"Yes sir," Parker said, then relayed the information on his radio.

Stanley headed toward the front door.

Cooper grabbed his arm. "Where are you going?"

"Inside." Stanley shook him off. "You and Jayla stay out here. Parker, nobody gets through this door but me. Do you understand?"

The officer nodded.

"Can't we go with you?" Cooper asked.

"Cop or not, that's an order," Stanley snapped. Drawing his gun, he strode to the front door.

Jayla could see that the lock had been forced. Part of the doorframe had splintered.

Stanley glanced at the upstairs windows, then pushed the door open and disappeared inside.

"What is he going to do?" Jayla asked, gripping the strap of her purse.

Cooper shook his head. "Bring him in, I hope."

They stood waiting and listening. Jayla could hear Stanley inside calling for the man to come out and give himself up. She didn't hear a response.

"But what if Stanley's in on it?" She grabbed Cooper's sleeve. "What if—"

A gunshot exploded, and then there was absolute silence.

There was another loud bang, but this one didn't sound like a gunshot. Jayla wasn't sure if it was a door slamming or someone trying to break down a door.

"Get up here, Parker!" Stanley bellowed. "Daniels! Kent!"

Cooper had already pulled his gun. "Stay down," he told Jayla. He followed Parker inside the apartment house.

Crouching low in the opening of the front door, she watched Cooper and the officers charge up the stairs. From her vantage point, she could see everything.

"Open the door!" Stanley ordered, shoving his shoulder against the door of the apartment. "Open up!"

There was no answer.

"Open it," Stanley told Kent.

Kent rammed the door a few times, and it finally opened.

Daniels and Parker stormed inside with their guns drawn.

"It's clear," Daniels called over his shoulder.

Stanley entered the apartment too.

Cooper let out a heavy breath and leaned over the stair rail. "You can come up," he said to Jayla. "It's over. He's dead."

She stood in the doorway, feeling strange about entering the building. When she walked inside the front door, she noticed the place was empty, stripped to the walls. There was a dead man upstairs. At least he wouldn't kill again. She squared her shoulders and headed up the stairs.

"He's not dead," Kent announced from the apartment.

"What?" Stanley asked. He sounded stunned.

Jayla reached the top of the stairs and steadied herself against the railing. She felt weak.

"He put a bullet in his brain," Stanley said. "How can he still be alive?"

"It happens," Cooper said. "Ask me how I know."

Gathering her courage, Jayla inched toward the open door of the apartment and peeked inside. The man was lying on the bare floor with a gun beside him. He was tall with an athletic build, and he had long, dark hair. She guessed he was about thirty-five. He wore a long-sleeved shirt and gloves, but Jayla didn't doubt his arms were covered with tattoos.

Kent tried to keep him from bleeding out, and Parker bolted down the stairs.

"Get everything we've got," Stanley ordered. "Daniels, call EMS out here now. Then contact forensics."

Cooper knelt down by the man and studied him, not touching anything.

Jayla put her purse on the floor and knelt beside him. "Does he have a chance?"

"Your guess is as good as mine." Cooper leaned close to the gun. "It's definitely just been fired," he said, sniffing it. "Ballistics will have to confirm it fired the bullet that hit him."

"There aren't any other weapons to choose from. He was in a locked room. It's the only gun here." Stanley motioned toward the man's damaged head. "That wasn't a wasp sting. Besides, he'll have residue on his right hand, judging from the entrance wound. Seems like a pretty clear case of suicide."

"*Attempted* suicide," Jayla corrected him.

"Is he still breathing?" Stanley asked Kent.

"Yeah." Kent glanced toward the door. "Where's Parker?"

"Here." Parker hurried into the room with the medical kit and dropped to his knees at Kent's side. "I heard another siren."

Parker opened the kit, and he and Kent did what they could to try to stop the bleeding.

Jayla moved to help.

But Cooper stopped her. "Let them do it. We need to keep from touching anything as much as possible." He nodded almost imperceptibly toward Stanley.

She understood. If Stanley was somehow involved in all this, they couldn't ruin any evidence that might tell them that.

In another minute, there were sirens outside, and then two EMTs rushed into the apartment. One of them took over for Kent and Parker while the other one herded everybody else to the other side of the room.

Stanley stood watching, arms crossed, until the paramedics had their patient stabilized and strapped to a gurney. "Go with them," he ordered Kent. "Don't let the guy out of your sight. He's in custody."

"Got it," Kent said.

By the time they transported the suspect out of the apartment, a forensics team was waiting to come inside.

"Is this purse part of the scene?" one of them asked.

"Sorry," Jayla said, walking over to the woman. "I think one of the EMTs must have pushed it out of the way when they were here."

The woman glared at her.

"It's okay," Stanley said. "I saw her bring it in. It's nothing to do with the case."

The woman snatched the purse and tossed it to Jayla. Then she started taking photographs.

Jayla knew processing a crime scene took hours and sometimes days. But she guessed this one would be relatively quick. They wouldn't have to wait for an autopsy before the scene could be released. Except for the gun and the physical evidence, there was very little to be documented. And the whole apartment house was empty. Eric had been the only one here before the police came.

Jayla noticed Stanley talking to another member of the forensics team. "There's not much to see anymore," she whispered to Cooper. "Should we go? Maybe we can stop by the hospital and see how the guy's doing."

"Not yet," Cooper said, his voice low. "I don't want to leave until Stanley does. He could have nothing to do with this, but I want to be sure. I'll tell you more later."

Finally, everything was done, and the forensics team left. Stanley sent Daniels to the hospital to back up Kent and told Parker to go down to the squad car.

"I was surprised you entered the apartment by yourself," Cooper remarked to Stanley as they started walking toward the stairs. "That was a pretty big risk, wasn't it?"

"I thought I could get up here without him realizing it," Stanley answered. "And I hoped I might be able to talk him into coming out without a fight. He never gave me a chance."

"That's too bad," Cooper said. "I would have been interested to know what he had to say. But he could still pull through."

Stanley snorted. "I wouldn't count on it. If he does make it, he probably won't ever be the same."

"I was worried about that myself last year," Cooper said, "but fortunately it didn't end up that way."

"Your gunshot wasn't through the middle of your head," Stanley said. "I guess that would make a difference."

"I had some great doctors too," Cooper added. "You never know what they can do."

"True enough. Well, I'm taking off. I need to stop at the station before I can go home." Stanley blew out a long breath. "I should have been off duty hours ago." He raised an eyebrow at Jayla. "Aren't you tired by now?"

"I am," she admitted. "There's nothing I'd rather do than sleep the rest of the night and all day tomorrow. Should we turn out the lights before we go?"

"They were on when we got here," Stanley said. "Better leave them." He hesitated at the bottom of the stairs, glancing around the empty house.

Cooper and Jayla stayed with him.

Finally, Stanley told them good night, and they went to their respective cars.

Cooper started the engine, but he didn't immediately pull into the street.

Jayla sat there with her purse in her lap, waiting for him to say or do something. "Aren't we leaving?" she asked him at last.

"Yeah, but I want to make sure Stanley doesn't have any reason to go back inside the building."

She tilted her head. "What do you think he's up to?"

"I don't know," he said. "Maybe he was supposed to make sure Eric didn't get out of there alive."

Jayla raised one eyebrow.

"First rule of assassination is to assassinate the assassin."

"What?"

"Let's suppose that somebody hired Eric to act crazy and claim he killed Kinner and Myers to take attention off the real killer," Cooper said. "What's the next logical step? The real killer needs to get rid of Eric, so Eric can take the blame for all the killings and can't deny anything."

"So you think Stanley killed him? It wasn't suicide?"

"I don't have a clue what happened in that apartment," he admitted. "Stanley took a big risk going in alone."

She shuddered. "Unless he knew the guy."

"Exactly."

Jayla noticed that Stanley hadn't driven off either. "What about the evidence?" she asked. "Wouldn't Eric have gunshot residue on his hand if he shot that gun? What about the weapon? Stanley still had his gun when you entered the apartment, didn't he?"

"Yeah, but it could have belonged to Eric," Cooper reasoned. "If not, I'd be willing to bet there's more than one cop who can get ahold of a throwaway if he happens to need one."

"And the residue?"

"Eric was wearing gloves," he said. "I'm betting the right-handed glove will have residue on it. But that doesn't mean that was the hand that pulled the trigger. If somebody wanted to make it look like suicide, he wears a glove, fires the gun, drops the gun near the body, and puts the glove on the victim's hand along with all the residue. Easy."

"Would Stanley have had time to do it?"

"He would have to be quick, but I think so," Cooper answered. "Let's say Stanley got Eric to let him into the room. It wouldn't be difficult. Eric knows him. In fact, he *works* for him. Stanley comes up behind Eric, shoots him in the head, drops the gun, puts the gloves on him, and hurries out. I heard another bang after the shot. Was that Stanley trying to break the door down? Or was he slamming the door after leaving the apartment?"

"I was wondering about that," Jayla said. She watched as Stanley finally pulled his squad car away from the curb. "So what now?"

"I'll take you back to the station so you can drive your car home."

"But what about Stanley?" she asked. "If he has residue on his hands, he's going to wash it off before anybody can test him for it. And if he was close enough to shoot Eric, he'd have residue all over his clothes."

"That's another reason we need to get to the station as soon as possible," he said. "Somebody has to check him out before he has a chance to go home."

"Why don't you call whoever's on duty?" she suggested. "Stanley might leave before we get there."

"I don't want to make a big deal of it," Cooper said. "I may be way out of line here. If Stanley did kill Eric and if he's responsible for tampering with the statements, stealing the 911 recording, leaving you that note, and hiring Eric to threaten you, then I want to know why. Was he paid off?"

"It's possible," Jayla said. "Did he have something to do with Jill's murder in the first place?"

He shook his head. "I would have recognized him that night. No way I would have forgotten that or gotten him mixed up with someone else."

"You could have done that with Eric tonight," she pointed out.

"Yeah." Cooper swiped one hand across his mouth. "Wolff is tall, and he has dark hair and eyes. I still might not be remembering clearly. Maybe I picked out Wolff because he was involved with Jill and he resembled the guy I glimpsed coming out of her apartment before I got shot."

"If that's the case, Eric is guilty, and Stanley didn't do anything," Jayla concluded.

"I don't know, but I have to check it out," he said. "I wish I could remember that night more clearly."

"It still bothers me that I can't recall more about the 911 call," she said. "I really thought working on this case with you would trigger some memories. Any little thing might help."

"Keep thinking. It'll come." Cooper pulled into the street. "Meanwhile, we'd better get to the station and take care of this with Stanley. He'll kill me if he's not involved."

"But he's a cop," Jayla said gently. "He'll understand."

One side of his mouth quirked up. "After he kills me."

She smiled. Then she rubbed her forehead and started rummaging in her purse. "I'm getting a terrible headache."

"Do you have something you can take?" Cooper asked, glancing over at her.

"Yeah, I have—" She frowned, digging deeper into her purse. "I don't see my keys."

"You didn't put them in your pocket or something?"

"These pants don't have pockets. It's very irritating. But I did put my keys in this front pocket of my purse. They must have fallen out when the forensics expert tossed it to me. I had my purse with me the rest of the time."

"We'll go back." He pulled up in front of the apartment house.

"I'll hurry," she said, opening the door.

"I'll go with you," Cooper offered.

"No, then you'll have to find a place to park, and it'll take too long," Jayla said. "I'll just run up and get my keys. I'll be back before you know it."

"Let me come with you," he insisted.

"The place is empty, isn't it? The lights are still on." The tree blocked her view of the window of apartment four, but she could tell there was still light coming from it. "It won't take a second. It'll be much faster than hunting for a parking space and walking a few blocks."

Cooper didn't seem convinced.

"Come on. There's nobody in there. It was checked out by a whole team of police officers not five minutes ago. Stanley and Eric are both gone. You can sit here and watch me." Jayla gestured toward the house. Through the lighted front windows, she could clearly see the stairway and the landing.

He sighed. "Okay. But if you're not back soon, I'm leaving the car in the middle of the street and coming after you."

She leaned over and gave him a peck on the cheek. "You worry too much. I'll be right back."

Jayla jumped out of the car and ran to the front door. It was shut, but she pushed it open easily and rushed up the stairs. The police had already taken Eric away. They'd seen Stanley leave. There was nothing in the house, no reason to feel nervous about being here alone, no reason to hurry, but she did anyway.

At the top of the landing, she turned to give Cooper a spirited wave, and then she headed toward the apartment. The quicker she did this, the quicker she'd be out of here and back in the car.

"Don't be silly," Jayla muttered under her breath as she reached to open the door. "There's no one here. Nothing to be afraid—"

Then someone laughed.

Jayla froze where she stood, holding her breath, hoping the pounding of her heart wasn't loud enough for anyone but her to hear. There *was* someone inside the apartment. She didn't know how that could be, but there was.

The voice was faint, but she could make out the words.

"I had to tell you things went well today," a woman said. "About that transaction we discussed. It was a great success."

Again there was that laugh, and this time Jayla recognized it.

Laurel Wolff.

It had to be her. But why was she here?

"Don't worry, Dane, mean lily scat," Laurel said. "Things will work out for us now. All will be well."

Jayla started to shake. She didn't understand what "mean lily scat" meant, but she knew she had heard it before. It popped into her head with perfect clarity. She had heard that phrase in the horrible voice used by Jill Kinner's murderer in the 911 call last year. The man had called Jill that before he killed her. What was it? A term of affection that had become a taunt? And how did Laurel know it unless she had learned it from him?

It was clear that Laurel didn't realize Jayla was outside the apartment. She was still talking to her husband. Jayla had to get down those stairs and out of the house before she was caught. The walk across the landing to the stairs stretched from feet into miles. No cover. Not even shadows. She couldn't make a sound. She had to at least get to where Cooper could see her. She had to let him know she was in trouble.

Jayla drew a deep, silent breath and took her first step toward the stairs. Then she froze again as the door behind her opened.

"Stop right there," Laurel ordered. Her voice was low and even, almost musical. "Turn around."

Jayla froze. She heard the telltale click of a gun being cocked. She rotated slowly on the spot. "How did you get here?" *Dear God, please help me.*

"You'd better come in," Laurel said, stepping back and motioning toward the door as if inviting Jayla in for tea. "We have a lot to discuss, don't we? I think a little girl talk will be just the thing."

"Cooper's out in the car waiting for me," Jayla said, not daring to disobey. "He's probably already on his way up."

"Go inside," Laurel ordered.

As Jayla entered the apartment, she noticed an opening in the drywall in one corner. It wasn't a large space, but she could see that part of the wall had been built out to make enough room for a chair. She hadn't paid much attention to the area before. It had appeared to be a space to accommodate ductwork or even an obsolete chimney.

"All this time, you were hiding in there and waiting for Eric to come," Jayla said. "You killed him and made it look like it was suicide."

Laurel shrugged. "I was done with him."

"What did he do?" Jayla asked, her mind whirling. "Was he the one who scratched Daryl Peters with those awful gloves while disguised as a woman?"

Laurel nodded.

"And he planted Daryl's DNA under Katie's nails to implicate him?"

"He did that and everything else I paid him to do."

"Did he also call and threaten me?" Jayla asked.

"Yes."

Jayla massaged her temples. "Why?"

"When it appeared the case against Daryl Peters might break down, I developed a backup plan," Laurel said smugly. "I got Eric to threaten you and your sister and have the police chase him here. He thought he was going to disappear. I told him if he would confess to the murders, I'd make sure he was never arrested for them. He believed I was going to smuggle him out of the country."

"So you killed him instead. Cooper will testify that he confessed, and your husband will be released."

"All I have to do is go home and wait for the call telling me that my husband needs a ride home."

"But Eric isn't dead," Jayla reminded her. "He'll tell the police everything."

"Come now. I knew what I was doing. If he's not dead already, he'll be nothing more than a vegetable. He's no danger to me. Not like you."

"You can't kill me," Jayla said, knowing perfectly well she could. "You couldn't possibly fake another suicide here."

"As soon as I get home, I'll take some potent sleeping pills. My housekeeper will testify that I took them and didn't move all night. If the police check on me, I'll still be in bed, with the pills in my system." Laurel smirked. "How you happened to be killed here after everyone left will end up being one of those unsolved mysteries they put on TV."

"Cooper's outside waiting for me," Jayla repeated. "If he hears a shot, he'll be right up."

"I'll see to him soon," Laurel said coolly. "But you first."

"Tell me one thing," Jayla said, trying to stall. *Cooper, please come.* "What is 'mean lily scat'?"

Laurel frowned slightly, then smiled. "*Min lille skat*? I learned that from my husband. His parents were Danish, and in their language it means 'my little darling.' Isn't it sweet?"

"I heard that phrase on the 911 call before your husband killed Jill Kinner," Jayla replied, her voice shaking. "It was horrible."

"She deserved it," Laurel spat. "He was through with her, and she was going to make a scandal about the whole thing if he left her."

"He cheated on you."

"He came back to me." Laurel raised the gun. "Now it's time to be finished here."

Cooper pushed the front door open barely wide enough for him to get through and crept up the stairs with his gun at the ready. He had caught a glimpse of Jayla on the landing, but then she had left his line of sight and headed toward apartment four. It was taking too long for her to retrieve her keys. He was certain something was going on.

Careful not to make a sound, he moved from the head of the stairs to the apartment door. It was open only a crack, and he could hear voices inside—Jayla's and . . . Laurel Wolff's?

Peering inside carefully, he saw that Laurel had a gun trained on Jayla. His heart wrenched. He couldn't lose her, not before he'd had a chance to tell her how he felt about her.

He kicked open the door. Two gunshots rang out—the one he fired toward Laurel and the one she fired toward the sound of his arrival. His shot hit Laurel's shoulder, spoiling her aim. Her shot hit the landing behind him.

Laurel fell to the floor, clutching her shoulder and sobbing.

Jayla snatched the gun that had flown out of the other woman's hands.

"Are you okay? Did she hurt you?" Cooper asked, afraid to take his attention off Laurel even for a second but unable to resist the temptation to check for himself that Jayla was unharmed.

"I'm fine," Jayla said, keeping the gun pointed at its owner. "You'd better get EMS out here again."

Just then there was the wail of sirens in the distance.

"I alerted the police when I realized you were in trouble," Cooper explained. "One of the officers can call an ambulance."

Laurel glared at him, her face streaked with tears and mascara. "I'm bleeding to death."

Jayla was still holding the gun on her.

Cooper put his own weapon far out of reach and knelt down at Laurel's side to examine the wound. There was a lot of blood, but the injury itself wasn't too bad. "The bullet hit the top of your shoulder. It made more of a groove than a hole. You should be fine. Physically at least."

Laurel continued to glower at him but said nothing.

"Before the cops get here, I want to know something," Cooper said. "Who is working for you at the station?"

Laurel clutched her shoulder and raised her chin defiantly.

He gave her a conspiratorial smile. "Come on now. You don't want to go to jail for this alone, do you?"

"All right. Yes, I paid someone off. Someone who tampered with the evidence, stole the 911 tape, and left the note for Jayla."

"Who?" *Not Stanley*, Cooper pleaded silently. *Please not Stanley*.

Laurel huffed. "It was that woman at the front desk. Sheila something or other. I found out her husband needed cancer treatment, and I knew she was desperate for money."

Cooper clenched his jaw, not wanting to give Laurel the satisfaction of seeing his shock. Poor Sheila. Maybe under the circumstances they wouldn't go too hard on her. Laurel had certainly known how to prey on her desperation. And he and Jayla had bought into Sheila's attempts to cover her own guilt by subtly implicating Stanley. The whole thing was a mess.

The sirens came closer and then stopped. A few moments later, the front door burst open.

"This is the police!" Stanley shouted. "Cooper, are you in there?"

"Yeah," Cooper called back. "We're all clear. Come on up."

Stanley burst into the apartment with Officer Parker on his heels.

"For crying out loud," Stanley said. "What's going on here?"

Laurel barely spared him a glance.

"Get the medical kit again," Stanley told Parker. "If there's anything left in it."

Parker disappeared out the door.

Stanley shook his head at Cooper and Jayla. "I can't leave you two alone for five minutes."

"Glad I caught you before you got all the way home," Cooper said, clapping him on the shoulder.

"Do you know what time it is?" Stanley demanded. "I haven't slept since five yesterday morning."

"I think we're done now," Cooper said. "Laurel had a pretty elaborate plan, and she almost got away with it."

Jayla gave Stanley a wicked little grin. "And we almost had you tangled up in it."

Stanley raised his eyebrows. "Me? What's that supposed to mean?"

By the time Cooper and Jayla had told Stanley everything that had happened and why they had suspected him of being part of it, the ambulance had arrived. The paramedics bandaged Laurel's shoulder and strapped her to a gurney.

"She's a wily one. I'm going along to keep an eye on her," Stanley said as he followed the gurney to the door. "I'm not taking any chances of her slipping out on us."

"My attorneys will have me out on bail before the hospital says I'm fit to go home," Laurel said imperiously.

"Don't count on it," Stanley told her. "I suspect you're going to spend a long time where nobody gets to wear designer clothes."

Laurel gave him a cool smile. "I'd bet you on that, but you couldn't afford the stakes." She pointed at Cooper and Jayla with her good arm. "And you both had better buckle up. Once my attorneys are through with you on the witness stand, you'll wish you'd kept your mouths shut."

"See you in court," Cooper said pleasantly.

Jayla fluttered her fingers at Laurel with a smile.

The paramedics carried her away.

"You're in charge until forensics arrives," Stanley told Parker. "After that, if they don't need you for anything, come pick me up at the hospital."

"Right," Parker said.

Stanley put his hands on his hips and faced Cooper and Jayla. "You two will have to make formal statements about all this."

Cooper nodded. "When you're wrapping up this case, you should check out a company called LL & Z Investment Properties. They're the ones who bought this apartment house and were having it remodeled."

"Why?" Stanley asked. "What's the connection?"

"I wouldn't be surprised if the company can be traced back to Dane and Laurel Wolff," Cooper explained. "Alison Travers is the managing partner, and I'd be willing to bet that she's dating one of Wolff's lawyers or something like that."

"You've got a point," Stanley said. "Now, you come see me bright and early. Got it?"

Cooper groaned. "It already *is* bright and early."

"Oh no," Stanley said with a grin. "It's early, but it's not bright yet."

As soon as the ambulance was gone, another patrol car pulled up in front of the house. It was Kelly's.

"Hey," Kelly said, bounding up the stairs as Cooper and Jayla were coming down. "What's going on here? Are you both okay?"

"Yeah, against all odds," Cooper said. "What are you doing here?"

"I heard everybody being dispatched out here, and I thought you were in trouble again. As usual." Kelly cocked his head. "Didn't they already get the guy earlier tonight?"

"They got the guy," Jayla said. "Now they have the woman behind it. Laurel Wolff."

"Wow," Kelly said. "You've got to be kidding me. Why did she do it?"

"She was trying to get her husband's charges dismissed." Cooper filled in his brother on everything that had happened. "She didn't care what she had to pay or who she had to hurt to do it."

"Or kill," Kelly said grimly.

"No, the guy wasn't dead when they took him away," Cooper said.

"He is now," Kelly said. "He died en route to the hospital. If you two hadn't come back here, Dane and Laurel Wolff would have gotten away with it. All of it."

They were quiet for a few moments as Kelly's words sank in.

"Did you find your keys?" Kelly asked, breaking the silence.

Cooper and Jayla exchanged glances.

"Oh my goodness, I totally forgot about them," she said. "I'll be back."

"Wait," Cooper told her, taking her arm. "This time we both go."

"Hang on." Kelly followed them. "I want to see the scene."

There was a marker on the landing, and Cooper stopped to examine it. He gave a low whistle. "That's where her bullet went."

"That's where you were shot before," Kelly said softly.

"But you were right the whole time," Jayla said, pressing closer to Cooper. "You did see Wolff leaving the apartment last year, and he was the one who shot you."

Cooper nodded. "He also killed Jill Kinner. Laurel hired Eric to kill Katie Myers to make it look like somebody besides her husband had killed Jill, and then she killed Eric."

"Only he wasn't Eric," Kelly said. "His name was Tony Barzelli. One of the cops at the hospital recognized him when the ambulance brought him in."

"Really?" Cooper asked. "Who was it?"

"Dunham was there with a suspect," Kelly continued. "It so happens that he was the officer who'd sent Tony to prison for five years for dealing meth. Tony hadn't been out long."

"Nice guy," Cooper said, putting more than a touch of sarcasm into his voice. "But it was a nasty way to go, no matter what he did. At least Dane and Laurel will be locked up for a long time."

"Good. No more threatening notes or phone calls," Jayla remarked. "I'll be able to sleep well again."

"You and Mary Ann both," Cooper said. "And Daryl Peters."

"Peters will be able to go home soon," Jayla said. "Ray Jensen will be glad to see him."

"Let's get your keys so you can go home and tell your sister the good news," Cooper said. He led the way to apartment four.

There were a number of police officers and forensics experts in the apartment, but none of them had seen a set of keys.

Cooper, Jayla, and Kelly checked where Jayla remembered setting down her purse, but there was no sign of anything in the bare room besides the bloodstains that had been left by Laurel and Eric.

"The keys aren't here," Cooper said finally. "Where else can they be?"

"We'll have to backtrack, starting with the walk from your car to the house," Jayla said.

With Kelly's help and by the bright light of his flashlight, they finally found the keys on the floorboard of Cooper's car.

"How did I not see them when I got out of the car?" Jayla asked. "Or hear them when they fell out of my purse?"

Cooper slipped one arm around her. "I guess things were meant to happen the way they did. Like Kelly said, if we hadn't gone back, the Wolffs would have gotten away with at least three murders."

"Thank God they didn't," Jayla said.

Cooper smiled at her. "Amen."

Kelly cleared his throat. "If you have everything you need, I'd better get back on patrol." With a wave, he jumped into his squad car and drove away.

Glad they were finally alone, Cooper smiled at Jayla. "Do you want me to drive you home? I can take you back to the station to get your car later."

"Thanks," she said. "I'm too exhausted to drive."

"Let's go," Cooper said, ushering her to the car.

When they arrived at Jayla's house, he escorted her to the front door. He wasn't surprised to see that Mary Ann had left the porch light on. He hesitated, not quite ready to let Jayla go after coming so close to losing her forever. "I'm so relieved that you're okay," he said softly, tucking a strand of her hair behind her ear.

Jayla wrapped her arms around his neck. "Thank you for saving my life. I was terrified."

"So was I," Cooper admitted, pulling her close. "But we both did what we had to do. And we're both fine." He grinned. "Besides, it's the least I could do for my partner."

She narrowed her eyes. "What's that supposed to mean?"

"We work well together, don't we? Now that we're on the same page again."

"Yeah, but I'm not sure what you're talking about."

"As a private investigator, I've realized that it's hard for me to do everything all by myself," he said. "So what do you think? Would you like to start helping me out on a regular basis?"

"I still have a job," Jayla reminded him.

"You can help me out on the side." Cooper pulled her a little closer. "Maybe we can eventually make it full-time." He touched his lips to hers. "On a very permanent basis."

Her long lashes brushed her flushed cheeks. "What do you mean?" she breathed.

He smiled. "You don't expect me to raise Lizzie all by myself, do you?"

Jayla pressed her cheek against his. "Working with you on this case was scary, but I'm glad we did what we had to do. I've been afraid way too long." She gazed into his eyes. "I was so afraid of losing you."

"I was wrong to believe that I could live without you," Cooper said. "I'm sorry for all the pain I put you through. I'll never leave you again. I promise I will always protect you." He trailed his finger down her cheek. "And always love you."

"Always?" she asked, and her eyes filled with tears.

"Yes." He kissed her again, warm and sweet, the way he'd wanted to kiss her all these months. Thank God she had given him another chance. He wouldn't take it for granted.

They broke the kiss and laughed when the porch light started flickering on and off.

"That's Mary Ann," Jayla said. "She learned that trick from our parents. It means we're supposed to say good night." She grinned. "I guess I should say good morning."

She was right. He could see the Dallas skyline silhouetted against the soft glow of dawn.

"I have a feeling she's going to burn out a lot of light bulbs that way," Cooper said, embracing Jayla. "But it'll be worth it."

And he kissed her again.